The 7th Woman

A Paris Homicide novel

Frédérique Molay

Translated from French by Anne Trager

LE FRENCH BOOK

First published in France as
La 7e femme
by Librairie Arthème Fayard
World copyright © 2006 Librairie Arthème Fayard

English translation copyright © 2012 Anne Trager
First published in English
by Le French Book, Inc., New York

www.lefrenchbook.com

Copyediting by Amy Richards
Cover designed by David Zampa

ISBNs:
978-1-939474-03-2 (trade paperback)
978-1-939474-96-4 (hardcover)
978-0-9853206-6-9 (Kindle)
978-0-9853206-7-6 (epub)

"Trials never show us the face we are expecting."
—François Mauriac

MONDAY

1

MARIE-HÉLÈNE

He couldn't breathe. His mouth was dry, and his throat tight. He was free-falling. She was wildly attractive: about thirty-five, five and half feet tall, slender, with short auburn hair and brown eyes highlighted by plain eyeglasses. Her voice was soft and steady. She had a keen, friendly, and reassuring look in her eyes, and a smile illuminated her face—a magnificent smile. He stared at her intensely, like a pimply teenager entranced by a *Playboy* cover girl.

"So, you're Mr. Sirsky, is that correct?" she asked. She was sitting behind her desk, her fingers absently playing with a pen.

He nodded.

"Nico Sirsky. Is your first name Nico?" she continued in a voice that was so memorable, he was sure he would distinguish it from all others from that moment on.

"Yes. It's not a nickname."

"When were you born?"

"January eleventh, thirty-eight years ago."

"What do you do?"

"I'm divorced."

What a strange answer, but it was the first one that came to mind when he looked at her. He had married too young—when he was twenty-two—and had fathered a child. He was single again and not particularly interested in women, except for an occasional roll in the hay. No woman had ever had this effect on him. He had thought these feelings were the stuff of novels and movies.

"Mr. Sirsky?" the young woman pressed.

He looked at her hands. No wedding ring.

"Mr. Sirsky!"

"What would you like to know?" he asked, suddenly sheepish.

"Your profession would be enough."

What an ass he was being.

"Chief of police."

"And more specifically?"

"Head of the Paris Criminal Investigation Division."

"Would that be the famous Brigade Criminelle at 36 Quai des Orfèvres?"

"That's right, La Crim'."

"I suppose it's a stressful job."

"Sure. But no more than yours, I guess."

She smiled. She was incredible.

"So, who sent you to see me—your brother-in-law, Dr. Perrin, right?" she continued.

Actually, it was his sister who had insisted, behaving like his mother.

"What exactly is wrong?"

"Not much."

"Please, Mr. Sirsky, let *me* be the judge of that."

"I've had a stomachache for about three months."

"Have you already seen a doctor?"

"Never."

"What does the pain feel like?"

"Burning," he said with a sigh. "And some cramps." It was out of character for him to admit any kind of weakness.

"Are you more anxious or tired than usual?"

He frowned. His work was weighing on him. He was waking up in the middle of the night, haunted by visions of bloody bodies. It was impossible for him to share the anxiety that assailed him. Who could he confide in? His colleagues? From time to time they did spend an evening together, joking about dead bodies to chase away the ghosts. But nothing could keep a cop grounded better than going home to a family and reconnecting with day-to-day life. Routine puts priorities into perspective so the day's sordid experiences can be forgotten. That was why he hired married men with children. Eighty percent of his staff met these criteria. They needed this balance to withstand the pressure of the cases his elite crime-fighting squad handled. He alone did not respect this rule.

"Mr. Sirsky, you haven't answered my question," the young woman said sharply.

He gave her a mulish look to make her understand that she wouldn't get any more out of him, and she changed the subject.

"Does anything calm the pain?"

"I tried eating, but that doesn't change a thing."

"Get undressed, and lie down on the table."

"Uh, totally undressed?"

"You can keep your underwear on."

He got up and obeyed. His tall and muscular build, blue eyes, and blond hair impressed women, but here he was a little uncomfortable. She approached him and put her hands on his flat stomach to examine him. He shivered. Erotic images raced through his mind.

"Is something wrong?" she asked.

"Medical examiners are the only doctors I know, and believe me they haven't made me want to be treated by any others," he responded, hoping she would believe him.

"I understand. However, some symptoms require that you see a specialist without delay. What do you feel when I press here?"

He didn't take his eyes off her. He wanted to take her in his arms and kiss her. Damn it. What was happening to him?

"Mr. Sirsky, if you don't help me out here, we won't get anywhere."

"Oh, sorry. What were you saying?"

"Where does it hurt?"

He put a finger on the middle of his abdomen, brushing the woman's hand. She palpated and then had him sit on the edge of the table to take his blood pressure. She returned to her desk. He didn't want her that far away.

"Get dressed, Mr. Sirsky. You are going to need some tests."

"What kind of tests?"

"One of them will be an endoscopy. The doctor will put an optical instrument down your throat to explore your digestive tract, and view your stomach lining and duodenum."

"Is that really necessary?"

"Absolutely. We need to determine the exact cause of your symptoms. It could be an ulcer. We can't treat you until we have a precise diagnosis. An endoscopic examination is not very pleasant, but it doesn't last long."

"Do you think it's serious?"

"There are several types of digestive ulcers. In your case, I think it is probably a duodenal ulcer, which is generally benign. Although it's usually caused by bacteria, stress and fatigue can make the symptoms feel worse. But we need to be sure. What do you do other than work?"

He thought for a while. "Run and play squash. And shoot, of course."

"You should slow down. Everyone deserves some rest."

"You sound like my sister."

"She gives good advice. Here's a prescription. Once you've had the endoscopy, make another appointment with my secretary."

"You're not going to do it?"

"A doctor in the department will do it."

He gave her another obstinate look.

"Is something wrong, Mr. Sirsky?"

"Listen, I'd like you to do it. Would that be possible?"

She looked at him calmly for a while. "Okay." She took out her appointment book and turned the ink-blackened pages.

"You look overbooked, and I'm adding to it," he said.

"Don't worry, we'll find a time. We have to do it quickly. Wednesday morning at eight. Will that work for you?"

"Of course. I'm not going to push my luck."

She stood and accompanied him to the door. There, her handshake was both caring and firm. He was sorry to leave. One final time, he read the nameplate affixed to the office door: "Dr. Caroline Dalry, professor of medicine, gastroenterologist, former Paris Hospitals chief resident."

Once he was outside Saint Antoine Hospital, the sounds of the city enveloped him, and he continued daydreaming about her delicate hands touching his stomach. A dull upper-abdominal pain brought him back to reality.

His cell phone vibrated on his hip. It was Commander Kriven, the head of one of the Criminal Investigation Division's twelve squads.

"We've got a customer," he said. "It's an unusual murder. You should come."

"Who's the victim?"

"Marie-Hélène Jory, thirty-six, white, assistant professor of history at the Sorbonne. Killed in her home, Place de la Contrescarpe in the Latin Quarter. Homicide with sexual connotations. The scene is particularly, well, shocking."

"Who found her?"

"Someone named Paul Terrade, her partner."

"He wasn't working?"

"He was, but the university was worried when she didn't show up for her class at one this afternoon. A secretary called his office, and he went home to see why she wasn't at work."

"Breaking and entering?"

"No signs."

Nico looked at his watch, which showed four-thirty. About two hours had elapsed since the discovery of the body. It was a miracle of sorts. Some evidence might still be intact, unless a lot of people had gone in and out of the apartment.

"I'll be right there."

"You don't really have a choice." Squad commanders were under orders to request his presence or his deputy's presence whenever they thought the situation was serious enough.

"And ask Dominique Kreiss to join us," Nico added. "Her input could be valuable."

She was a criminal psychologist with the Regional Police Department, recently hired for a brand new profiling unit. She wasn't there to take over any investigations, but rather to provide detectives with her psychological expertise. Considering what Kriven had described, it seemed logical to have her at the scene. She specialized in sexually related murders.

"Can't we call in the old bearded shrink?" Kriven grumbled. "That brunette's cute little ass distracts me!"

"Get your mind out of the gutter, would you, Kriven?"

"Impossible with the body she's got."

"I'm hanging up now. I don't want to hear any more of that crap. See you in a few."

The Latin Quarter reminded him of his childhood. His grandparents had a shop on the Rue Mouffetard. He recalled the days he spent playing with the kids of other shop owners on the street, which wasn't far from Saint Ménard Church. That kind of neighborhood conviviality was long gone now.

These days, the Place de la Contrescarpe was a tourist haunt because of its cafés. As Nico approached, he saw café customers gawking at the building, where an unmarked police cruiser, its lights flashing, was blocking the entrance. A man was slumped over the Renault's backseat. Two uniform officers were guarding the car. You could tell by their determined look they had no intention of letting the guy get away. David Kriven walked out of the building to meet Sirsky.

"We're lucky, Chief," he said. "The precinct officer had the good sense to evacuate everyone before he contacted us. It's all clean."

He meant that no other police units had been able to go over the crime scene before being told that the case was outside their jurisdiction. Too often, evidence was ruined by the time La Crim' was called in. Sometimes the body had already been removed. Those were not easy investigations. Yes, things were improving, but there was still a long way to go. To get the job done right, they really needed an efficient cop, which they had today.

"Where is this prodigious one?" Nico asked.

"On the third floor, standing in front of the apartment door. He's monitoring who's going in and out."

The two men walked up the stairs slowly. Nico studied the walls with each step to soak up the atmosphere.

"I showed up at three," the officer guarding the door said, as he shook the chief's hand. "I discovered the body and immediately knew that this wasn't an ordinary case."

"Why is that?" Nico asked.

"The woman, uh, well, what's been done to her... It's disgusting. I'll be honest. I couldn't even stay near her. It's enough to upset anyone."

"Don't worry," Nico said. "We all wind up being affected. Anyone who says otherwise is just showing off."

The officer nodded and let them through. Nico took the usual precautions to preserve any evidence, as did David Kriven.

Each of the division's squads had six members. The third-ranking member—there was an established order, based on experience and the role each member played—was the one responsible for the procedural aspects of working the crime scene. Pierre Vidal had waited for Chief Sirsky before he started collecting and sealing the evidence. He usually worked alone. For this investigation, he would do his job under the watchful eyes of Kriven and Sirsky.

The three detectives entered the living room. The victim lay on a thick cream-colored carpet.

"Shit. No," Nico let slip, despite himself. He squatted near the body and said nothing more. What could he say? The epitome of horror was spread out in front of him. Did man's perversity have no limits? He couldn't hold back a retch. He looked at his colleagues, all of whom were pale.

"See if Dominique Kreiss is here," he ordered.

Kriven averted his eyes from the body, and Chief Sirsky told the detectives to step out momentarily to give them a break.

"Go on. Now," Nico commanded.

Commander Kriven and Captain Vidal left the apartment, relieved.

Squatting beside the young woman, Chief Sirsky slowly took in the scene. The torture had been intense, the kind to make you lose your mind before you die. He thought about the probable unfolding of the murder and the killer's profile. He presumed that it was a lone man. He felt it. He knew it. Every emotion left him, which always happened to him at a crime scene. His work required focus, even in the most gruesome cases. But now his stomach was burning again. He was letting this murder get to him, and he would have to calm down. But how could he not react to this level of atrocity? Then Dr. Dalry's face came to him. She was smiling and holding out her hand, so gentle. She touched his cheek. He wanted to kiss her so much. He got nearer and nearer...

The apartment door opened, and Chief Sirsky heard steps in the hallway. David Kriven was leading the squad in. The psychologist followed. She was small, thirty-two years old, with bright, mischievous green eyes. Dominique Kreiss crouched next to the chief. The professional in her surveyed the site without blinking. She looked unaffected by the repugnant vision and the smell of death. Dominique Kreiss had a degree in clinical criminology and was a specialist in sexual assault. She wanted to fit right into the mainly male team of detectives working at 36 Quai des Orfèvres. If for no other reason than that, she never showed any weakness in front of her colleagues.

"Any level-headed person would take one look at this and run away," Nico said to the psychologist.

Their eyes met. Nico had built strong walls, and it was not easy to guess his weaknesses. But he knew Dominique Kreiss perceived the discomfort in his eyes.

"Nothing seems to have been moved," Nico said. "Everything is in order. It was not a burglary. I bet we will not find a single fingerprint. The work is meticulous and organized, and it is not some passing folly. There was no break-in, so the victim either knew the murderer or trusted him and let him in."

"How high a risk was this for the criminal?" Dominique asked.

"Pretty high. The Place de la Contrescarpe is very busy. Killing someone in her home without attracting attention, taking the time to clean up, and leaving as if nothing happened require a lot of control. This bastard works like a professional."

"The bastard, you say. You're right that it's probably a lone man, someone who is sure of himself enough to think that no one would notice him. He is methodical and calculating—the opposite of an impulse killer, who would have left evidence everywhere."

Nico nodded.

"Now, the victim," he said.

Dominique evaluated the mutilated, bloody body. Her heart rate quickened. "There's a mix of sex and violence. This is all about fantasy. I'd say that sex is not the motive. There is certainly a desire to demonstrate his power, to dominate her to the point of taking her life."

"Be more specific," Sirsky ordered.

Marie-Hélène Jory was lying naked on her back, her arms raised and pulled back, her wrists attached to a heavy coffee table.

"The bondage has pornographic overtones," Dominique said. "The victim was stabbed in the belly, certainly after suffering those lacerations."

"Jesus," Nico said. "Okay, Dominique, let's get down to the heart of the matter."

"Her breasts were amputated, and the criminal probably took them with him."

"What do you make of that?"

"The person who did that has a problem with his mother. Maybe he was abused or abandoned as a child."

Nico stood up, and the psychologist followed suit.

"You can start," the chief told Kriven and Vidal. "Keep the knot whole when you cut the rope. We'll want to examine it."

Vidal took latex gloves out of his field bag and handed pairs around. Then he began a methodical examination. He took a number of pictures and recorded his comments on a tape recorder. He tried to uncover every possible piece of evidence, every possible fingerprint, some sort of signature, voluntary or involuntary. Finally, he did a drawing of the room and made sure that everything was noted: the position of the furniture, the objects, and the body. In the meantime, Chief Sirsky encouraged David Kriven to search the apartment.

Dominique Kreiss slipped out. For now, there was nothing more that she could do.

2

THE INVESTIGATION BEGINS

They didn't finish until evening. The body was removed and taken to the medical examiner's office at the Paris Institut Médico-Légal, the morgue on the Quai de la Rapée. The public prosecutor's office would order an autopsy. Chief Sirsky decided to go back to headquarters to question Paul Terrade. Commander Kriven took off to help the fifth and sixth squad members, who were responsible for canvassing the neighbors. They had already started their rounds in the victim's building and in the cafés on the square. Perhaps they would uncover some leads.

Nico took the Boulevard Saint Michel to the Seine and then followed the river toward the Pont Neuf, which he crossed to reach the Île de la Cité. Dating from 1891, the building at 36 Quai des Orfèvres stood with the Palais de Justice, which housed the courts. Next to them were the government administrative offices at the Préfecture de Police, and nearby the Hôtel-Dieu hospital and Notre Dame Cathedral. It had always served as headquarters for France's elite police forces. Nico Sirsky was a member of the country's top crime-fighting organization, and he was proud of it. What more could he aspire to?

Deputy Police Commissioner Michel Cohen was waiting for him. It was seven-thirty in the evening, but the head-quarters were bustling as though it were the middle of the day. Crimes and misdemeanors would never adjust to France's thirty-five hour workweek. From the top of his five-feet-four frame, Cohen managed to assert his authority over all of his teams. Subtle and pernicious political games often got the better of the building's occupants, and turnover was high. Every kind of partisan grudge and broken career was possible here. Cohen was a top-notch professional who kept his political leanings to himself. He had moved up the ranks at the Quai des Orfèvres, starting his exemplary career in vice. For the last five years, he had held the reins of Paris's central criminal investigation division. Rumor had it that he had refused a national-level position because he wanted to stay out of politics, especially after the last elections, which had brought about multiple changes in the administration.

Cohen had left his third-floor office to join Nico Sirsky in his quarters on the fourth floor. Cohen had a lean frame, bushy black hair, a prominent nose, thick eyebrows, and keen eyes. He impatiently lit one of the large cigars he regularly smoked. The pungent white smoke immediately attacked Nico's throat, but Cohen took no notice.

"So, my boy," he said with his usual enthusiasm. "Hard at it, as always?"

They had an age difference of thirteen years, and Cohen had always treated him with manly affection. Nico was his protégé, almost like a son. Everyone knew it and sometimes joked about it. But Nico had forged a real reputation for his rigor, his hard work, and his abilities as a detective and leader. He had jealous colleagues to spare. He was only thirty-eight and already chief of police. Obviously, tongues wagged.

"I talked to our shrink, Kreiss," the deputy commissioner went on. "I see two possibilities. Either the crime scene is a trap, orchestrated by someone close to the victim and designed to make us think it's the work of a psychopath, or the murderer really is a nutcase who has nothing to do with the victim and won't stop there. In any case, it's not an incidental crime by a prowler. It was organized down to the tiniest detail."

Nico agreed. Cohen liked to summarize the information brought to him and, above all, to show that he was one step ahead of everyone else. He was the boss, and no one could say otherwise.

"Apparently it was not a pretty sight," he concluded, as if he wanted to make sure his colleague had gotten over it.

"The girl was subjected to a lot," Nico responded. "I just hope she died quickly."

"This case is a priority. Professor Vilars is on it. We'll have her report tonight."

Professor Armelle Vilars ran the medical examiner's office. She was a seasoned professional who left nothing to chance. Nico was glad to know that she was handling the case, and Cohen certainly shared that opinion.

"The boyfriend, Paul Terrade, is in the building," Nico said. "I'm going to question him. Kriven's team is out in the field, piecing together the victim's last day, beginning from when she got out of bed this morning. We'll find out what she did, where she went, and whom she met. That will give us a start."

"Good," said Cohen. "Follow that for the time being. This homicide is unusual, to say the least, so keep me in the loop. The public prosecutor wants you to call him tonight."

"Of course. Consider it done," Nico answered in a voice that he hoped sounded calm.

His boss was testing him. He could feel it. Would he be able to solve such an atypical crime quickly? It was quite a challenge for the person Cohen considered a worthy successor. Politics didn't affect him much, but he didn't have a simple relationship with the justice system.

French magistrates, including the public prosecutor, tried to wield authority over criminal investigators. Not so long ago, a magistrate had ordered an operation without explaining his reasons, the police commissioner had kept his men out of it and was subsequently sacked. Power struggles sometimes countered efforts to be efficient.

Cohen slapped Nico on the back—with a vigor the chief was used to—and returned to his office. Nico called the prosecutor and described the sordid details of the crime scene, and the latter ordered an investigation. In a few days, the state would designate a special magistrate to lead the inquiry. In the meantime, the prosecutor wanted to be kept informed. The procedure was complex but designed to make sure that all the rules were followed, and the rights of the accused were protected.

When Nico hung up, he asked his staff to bring Paul Terrade in. It was rare for him to question a witness himself. Usually the squad leader heading the investigation did it. But this was no ordinary case, and he had to be more involved. His troops wouldn't expect any less of him.

The victim's companion was five foot nine and nearing forty. His face was pale and his eyes red. Nico noticed the man's hands were shaking. Usually, one detective did the questioning, and if he couldn't get the person to talk, he'd bring in another detective and leave the room. Sometimes two of them would be in the room, but never more, and they never used physical force, even with the worst criminals. He had heard of that rule being broken only once. Guy Georges, the infamous Beast of the Bastille serial killer, was hit when he was arrested in 1998, after he had raped and killed at least seven women. No handcuffs were used at the headquarters either, a policy widely criticized after a suspect committed suicide. The man, Richard Durn, had carried out the Nanterre massacre in March 2002, opening fire at a city council meeting. Even though the no-handcuffs policy had been kept in place after the suicide, bars had been added to the windows.

"What happened?" Paul Terrade was sobbing. "Why was she killed? Why did they hurt her?"

His questions seemed really naive, Nico thought, but this naiveté was no guarantee of innocence.

"I have every intention of finding out," the chief responded. "You have just experienced a terrible trauma. I suggest that you see a doctor. If you want, we can give you something in the meantime. Perhaps there is some family to inform?"

"Yes. Marie-Hélène's parents are in Paris, and she has two brothers who live outside the city. She's got her grandmother, too. And there's my family."

"We will help you contact them after our talk, okay?"

Paul Terrade nodded.

"Do you have a place to sleep? You will not be able to go home immediately. Your apartment has been sealed off until further notice. Do you understand?"

"My sister lives close by. She'll put me up."

"Perfect. I don't want you to be alone," Nico said. "Do you have any idea of how this could have happened?"

Paul Terrade started sobbing, and tears ran down his sunken cheeks. He managed to get out a barely perceptible "no."

"Did your companion have any enemies? Or do you?"

"Not at all."

"Were you having an affair?"

"No!" Paul Terrade responded sharply, evidently shocked.

"And Ms. Jory?"

"Absolutely not! We had been living together for four years. Everything was going well. We wanted to start a family. She is a good teacher. Very conscientious. She never missed a class, that's why they called me."

Paul Terrade didn't know whether to talk about her in present or past tense. That was nearly always the case. Relatives needed time to comprehend this kind of loss.

"It was the first time the school ever contacted me. I was worried and went home to check on her. She was there. I saw her right away. She... she..."

"I can imagine what a shock it was. She died an atrocious death. Only a monster could have committed such an act. Perhaps it was someone you know."

"Impossible. We're just ordinary people."

"No money problems?"

"None. We both earn a decent living."

"And the family? Any particular concerns?"

"No. None. Really. I don't know what I can tell you."

"Often things are very simple. It could be someone you know, who maimed the victim to make it look like the work of a demented stranger."

"I can't believe that. Everyone loved Marie-Hélène. She was so nice. She was generous. She always thought about others."

His voice was choked. The man seemed sincere. Nico's first instinct was to trust him, but he knew from experience that he needed to be suspicious and keep up his guard. A murderer who was so sadistic could be capable of fooling anyone.

"You can help us," Sirsky said.

Terrade gave him a hopeful look.

"By giving us a detailed list of all family members, friends, and colleagues."

"Of course, I'll do that."

"There is nothing else you can do for the time being. Give us the address where you will be staying and a phone number, and I'll need to see you again. For now, my staff will contact your sister and ask her to come and get you. I am really very sorry for your loss."

Paul Terrade slouched under the weight of his pain. Then the two men stood up and said good-bye.

§ § §

Marie-Hélène Jory didn't have any classes in the morning and had taken her time getting dressed. Paul had left home around eight-thirty and had gone directly to his office. Witnesses confirmed that he was at his desk at nine. He needed thirty minutes to get to work by car. Commander Kriven checked it personally, with a stopwatch in hand. Around ten, Miss Jory went out to buy a paper and some bread. She had made the usual small talk with the shop owners. One of her neighbors, an elderly lady, crossed paths with her a little later, as she was re-entering the building. It was impossible to find out anything from that moment on. Had she met someone in the stairwell? Had she opened the door for a visitor? There were still unanswered questions. In any case, nobody had forced the door. A team of investigators continued to question the neighbors. Perhaps someone had seen her through a window. Kriven shared his boss's feeling that they wouldn't get any serious information from canvassing the area. He decided to return to headquarters and write up the victim's schedule, a document that was needed for the case file.

§ § §

The Criminal Investigation Division was organized like a pyramid. Twelve squads served under four section heads, who were either deputy chiefs or operational commanders. They took orders from the division chief and his deputy chief. These hundred or so civil servants, including about fifteen women, were the life force of the famous Crim'. The deputy commissioner supervised this division—as well as the gang, juvenile protection, vice, organized crime, and narcotics divisions—and above him was the commissioner. Two people were higher up: the police prefect and the interior minister. Although Nico Sirsky handled the gamut of major crimes, including terrorist threats—which were on the rise—kidnappings, and missing persons, the lion's share of his job involved investigating and solving homicides.

At nine that night, Commander Kriven reported to Sirsky's office with his superior, Deputy Chief Jean-Marie Rost.

"Were you able to put together Marie-Hélène Jory's schedule?" Nico asked.

"Yes, but there's nothing in it," Kriven said angrily as he handed over his report. He was always irritable when an investigation wasn't making progress. "Nobody saw or heard anything. It's useless. It's swarming with people there in the afternoon—people who live there, visitors, gawkers, tourists, but nobody gives a shit about anything! Anybody could do anything and not get any notice."

"That's to be expected, David," Jean-Marie Rost said. "Our men have started to question the victim's family, friends and colleagues and her boyfriend's. Tomorrow, I'll contact their bank and their doctors."

"What about forensics?" Nico asked. "What do our specialists have to say about the rope and the knot?"

"Nothing yet," Rost answered. "They are over-whelmed. Tomorrow is another day."

"Eight o'clock. My office. Shaved and ready to go back to work," Nico said sharply. "I want to keep a close eye on this case."

Moments after the two men had left the chief's large office, the telephone rang. It was the deputy public prosecutor's secretary.

"You have an appointment tomorrow morning at eleven with the state prosecutor," she said. "An investigating magistrate will be appointed later."

Perfect. That would give Rost enough time to put together the investigation report specifying how the body was found, along with what the witnesses and neighbors had said, the specifics of where the crime occurred, the weapons discovered on the premises, and any special evidence. They would have to add the full autopsy report and the photos of the victim that Professor Vilars would take.

The phone rang again. Speak of the devil.

"Nico? It's Armelle. Apparently you want to be there for Marie-Hélène Jory's autopsy. I just got the court order. I will be able to start in half an hour, just the time it will take you to get here. I should have been home hours ago to play model wife and mother. The bodies are piling up, and I'm not allowed to hire additional staff. Anyway, I didn't call you to complain. Are you on your way or not?"

Professor Armelle Vilars was a fiery redhead with a sharp wit. Nico appreciated her professionalism and attention to detail.

"I'll be right there."

The division dispatched an officer to attend every autopsy and report the medical examiner's analysis. Professor Vilars then sent her conclusions to the state prosecutor.

When Nico arrived at Quai de la Rapée, he was led to the room where the specialist was waiting. She and her assistant were ready to start. The two of them were wearing identical white tops, masks, and surgical gloves. Armelle Vilars winked at Nico and began working without any preamble.

Nico was used to this kind of scene. Nothing disturbed him—not the medical examiner's procedures, the exposed organs, the blood, or the smell of the ravaged body. Was he insensitive? The nature of his job demanded professional detachment. But the images did haunt him. It was impossible to erase them. He had to live with them.

Professor Vilars recorded her observations as she proceeded with the autopsy.

"The general appearance of the victim is that of a healthy woman who seems to have exercised regularly. She has little body fat. Body height is five feet six inches. Blood is being sampled for typing and DNA testing. Her hair is being combed for trace evidence. Nothing. There are thirty similar blunt-force wounds on the torso that I am measuring. Molds will also be taken to determine if they were made by the same weapon, more specifically, a whip, and, above all, if the same person inflicted the wounds. We will compare strips of skin to analyze impact and angles. There is a penetrating wound near the navel. The blade is deep, damaging vital organs. I am removing the knife and sending it to forensics as evidence. I am photographing all the wounds. Now for Miss Jory's hands: nail clippings are being taken and will be examined. Maybe she had some contact with her attacker, but I'm not hopeful. Now I'm taking ultraviolet shots that could reveal any invisible bruising on the body, and show any saliva, sperm, or fingerprints on the skin. Are you okay, Nico?"

He jumped. He was so focused, it felt as though he had been holding his breath since the beginning of the autopsy. Fatigue was gaining on him.

"Nico?" the medical examiner said again.

"Yes. I'm okay."

"Fine. I'll continue. The breasts were amputated with a scalpel. The technique was sophisticated. The thorax and abdomen are being opened, using a vertical incision from the xiphoid process to the pubis. I'm removing the organs one after the other, from top to bottom. There is no water in her lungs. I'll analyze her stomach and intestinal contents later, which should give me her time of death. I'm reaching the pelvic zone. I will examine bladder content later. Now the genitalia. Her uterus has increased volume. The victim was pregnant. No doubt about it."

"Pregnant?" Nico said. "How far along?"

"About a month," the examiner said. "There's a rough placenta and amniotic cavity. Forensics can do a paternity test with DNA identification."

Nico felt himself shiver.

"We'll examine the head next," Professor Vilars continued. "I'm opening the eyes. The corneas are cloudy, but I can still make out her brown eye color. There are traces of ether around her mouth, so he started by knocking her out. I see duct tape adhesive on her lips and skull. She couldn't scream. Now you know how the victim was neutralized. There are no contusions under the hair. The skull is being opened, first by cutting the skin from one ear to the other, and the brain is being inspected for blood clots."

Armelle Vilars finished her job.

"I'm seeing the public prosecutor at eleven," Nico said.

"The autopsy report will be on his desk. I'll send you a copy by e-mail, with details about the wounds, tox and blood results, stage of pregnancy, my conclusions, and impressions about the time of death and the nature of the weapon."

He had nothing to add. He left feeling like he was in a waking nightmare. Marie-Hélène Jory was expecting a child. He imagined his son, Dimitri, a strong four-teen-year-old, a joy. He sighed and then grimaced as a dull pain in his upper abdomen brought him back. His thoughts shifted to Dr. Dalry. He suddenly wanted to see her. She would know how to distract him and take him far away from these sordid stories.

His cell phone rang again. It was Tanya.

3

PERSONAL BUSINESS

"It's nearly midnight, Nico," his sister said, sounding worried. "Are you still working?"

"It's been a hard day. I'll be going home soon."

"You could have let me know what the doctor said."

Her maternal tone amused him. Tanya was two years younger than he was, but she was instinctively protective of him. What would he do without her?

"I'm really sorry, but I didn't have time."

"In any case, I know exactly what she said. Alexis talked to Dr. Dalry."

Dr. Alexis Perrin was his brother-in-law, first of all, and, on rare occasions, his primary-care doctor.

"What about doctor-patient privilege?" he asked, trying to get her angry.

"You can complain all you want to Mom," she said in a teasing voice.

Their mother, Anya Sirsky, was Russian. Her parents had fled their homeland in 1917, and she took pride in her roots. Still, she had married a Sirsky, who was Polish. Even though he had lived in France for quite some time, her Russian ancestors must have turned over in their tombs when she married a Pole! She was tall and thin, with long blond, nearly white hair, a strong personality, and acting skills in the purest Slavic tradition. She could shift from laughter to tears in seconds. Anya loved Griboyedov, Pouchkine, Lermontov, and Gogol and could recite entire passages written by her favorite authors. All his life, Nico had listened to her do so in the slightly gravelly voice that was distinctly her own. Nico smiled affectionately at this mention of their colorful mother.

"At least call me on Wednesday, when you have the results of the endoscopy. Don't forget that I'm your sister, and I worry about you. Who else would bother?"

Tanya never missed a chance to hassle him about his bachelorhood.

"Do you know Dr. Dalry?" he dared to ask, trying to sound detached.

"She went to medical school with Alexis, and they've stayed in touch. Why?"

"No reason."

"No reason? I doubt that. First of all, I know you, and you generally don't waste your time asking meaningless questions. Second, you are my brother, and I am still waiting for you to show some serious interest in a woman."

"Tanya, your imagination is way too active. I just wanted to make sure I was in good hands."

"The best. You know Alexis. For that matter, are you free for dinner on Thursday?"

"Sure. But please spare me the latest young woman you've found for me to meet."

His sister let out an exaggerated sigh. "Promise," she said, adding a hint of defeat. "Now get home and go to bed. And call me on Wednesday."

Nico returned to his home on the Rue Oudinot in Paris's seventh arrondissement. He opened the blue porte cochère between the French Overseas Territories Ministry and the Saint-Jean Clinic. A garden in the middle of the city opened before him. A few ivy-covered homes with flowers lined a small private alley. In the distance, he could see the Montparnasse Tower all lit up. Here, he was in the very heart of the capital, and yet there was no noise. He would never have had the means to pay for this without the money his father had left him. Thanks to a combination of hard work, intuition, and a bit of luck, his family had made a fortune in trading, and Nico had often lent a hand. The inheritance had allowed him to do the police work he loved without any financial constraints. The day he could no longer put up with the intense demands of his job, he could leave the police and live comfortably.

He unlocked the front door and immediately felt a presence. One of the three windows on the first floor was open. He pulled out his weapon, which he carried in a holster on his right side. He crept in the shadows. A small hallway opened onto the dining room and the kitchen. He decided to take the stairs to the second floor, which had a comfortable living room, his bedroom, and an adjacent bathroom. He slipped out of his shoes before climbing the first step. He heard a vague breathing. He was sure someone was there. When he reached the top step, he let out a sigh of relief. His son was sleeping in his pajamas on the black sofa.

Nico holstered his pistol and quietly approached the teenager. His son looked so much like him, he could have been a younger clone. He had a long, muscular body, re-fined features, deep blue eyes, and blond hair that needed a trim. The boy had a room and a bathroom on the third floor, next to the office. Nico decided not to wake him up, grabbed a plaid throw, and covered him up. He climbed up a flight and saw that his son's things were scattered across the floor, and his book bag was emp-tied on the bed. Nico and his ex-wife shared custody of Dimitri, and this was not his week. He was ready to bet that, once again, mother and son had fought. Sylvie held it against Dimitri that he looked so much like his father. She couldn't help it. She resented her son's affection for his father. She wanted her son's exclusive love. What else could Nico do but try to smooth things out between the two of them? He knew that it was important that they get along. He even discouraged Dimitri from moving in with him permanently. Not that he didn't want him to, but because Sylvie couldn't handle it. He decided to call his ex-wife.

"Nico?" he heard her say.

"Yes, it's me," he responded. "He's here. Don't worry. I would have called you earlier, but I just got back. He fell asleep on the couch."

There was silence on the other end.

"Sylvie, are you there?"

"Yes, I'm here," she said, sounding distraught. "I just don't know what to do with him anymore."

Her trembling voice announced a storm. Sylvie broke down easily.

"It's not the first time this has happened," Nico said. Step back a little. Give him some slack. You'll see. Things will go better."

"I'm not so sure about that. You're everything to him."

"Don't start that again. We've talked about this a thousand times. It's true that he and I are close, but you're his mother. He loves you, and he needs you."

"I don't know. I just don't know."

She was crying. He had to stay calm to keep things from getting any worse.

"This shared custody thing..."

"Listen, Sylvie, I won't ever question that. I promised you. So stop pummeling yourself with those stupidities. Take a vacation with Dimitri, and talk things over. In any case, I'll send him back to you tomorrow. It's your week. In the meantime, go to bed. I'm doing the same."

"Okay," she said in a whiny voice.

He ended the call and returned to look at his son sleeping peacefully. He leaned over and kissed him on the forehead. Then he went to his room, removed his holster from his belt, and put his gun in the safe. He took a long shower and climbed under the sheets. It was nearly one in the morning. As soon as he closed his eyes, he saw Marie-Hélène Jory's body. First it was in her apartment, in the middle of the living room. Then it was in the refrigerated morgue. The medical examiner's incisions were superimposed over the attacker's wounds. A dangerous psychopath. A criminal who took pleasure in his victim's terror. He was sure there would be more murders.

He fell asleep with this anxiety-ridden certainty.

TUESDAY

4

THE DAY AFTER

The night was an ordeal. Marie-Hélène Jory came back to life, only to be killed again as he stood by, incapable of making the slightest move. He watched her writhe in agony as an unknown masked man tortured her. Then she died, staring at him. In another dream, Dr. Dalry appeared, gentle and attentive. He wanted to hold her but couldn't. He woke up several times and drank a glass of milk to calm the heartburn gnawing at him.

Finally unable to go back to sleep, Nico got up and left early for his appointment at eight with Rost and Kriven. Two uniformed police officers wearing bulky bulletproof vests guarded the area around the division headquarters. One opened the red and white gate that led to a small parking lot squeezed between the imposing building and the traffic on the Quai des Orfèvres. He pulled into his reserved parking spot and went directly through the security checks, where the officers addressed him with a respectful, "Good morning, Chief." His steps echoed in the tiled hallway that led to the interior court-yard. He followed the outside wall on his left to the glass doorway leading to the division's offices. He climbed the famous three flights of black linoleum-covered stairs. The walls had lost their cream color and looked dirty. The premises were cramped and ramshackle—as if they were from another age and hardly worthy of a division such as the one he commanded. How long had they been promising a renovation? Visitors who were well aware of the division's impressive reputation were always shocked by this state of disrepair.

Nico entered his office, one of the few decent-sized rooms on that floor. The furnishings and colors were all dated, but he had the space he wanted and, above all, a view of the Seine. The inevitable portrait of the president reigned over a small sideboard across from the door. He settled into the brown leather chair in front of a huge desk piled with papers, including complaints filed the night before, pending cases, and an assessment of terrorist risks related to events in the Middle East. He quickly scanned them until Jean-Marie Rost and David Kriven arrived for their appointment.

The commander looked haggard. He handed his superior officer a bag of fresh croissants. Nico helped himself without hesitating. The upper-abdominal pain was still there.

"You look exhausted, David," Nico said.

"I couldn't get this case out of my head all night," the commander said.

He was, of course, talking about Marie-Hélène Jory's murder. Nico gave him an understanding look. He hoped his colleague would learn to leave his work behind when he went home, although he knew that wasn't likely. Even after several years on the beat, the images had a way of coming back. You would go over the interviews again and again. You would have doubts and wade through terrible nightmares.

"I'm sorry, David."

"You looked fried yourself."

There was no need to respond. Who could remain indifferent when faced with torture and murder? What surprised Nico was the amount of distress that Commander Kriven was exhibiting. He was a showoff some of the time, but deep down, he was just a cop, like the others.

"You'll see, David. It gets easier with age," he said, winking at Deputy Chief Rost to conclude the exchange. Commander Kriven didn't believe him but looked grateful. Nico slapped him on the shoulder, and they relaxed a little.

"The interview with Paul Terrade didn't provide anything useful," Nico said. "He doesn't appear to have anything to do with what happened and seems to be telling the truth. His girlfriend was one month pregnant, and we need to find out if Terrade was the father."

"That's horrible!" Kriven said.

"I know. Terrade didn't say anything about it. Does he know? Did she know? This is what we need to find out this morning. Rost?"

"I'll join Théron's squad to speed things up. Today we need to see the couple's doctors, go to the bank to go over their accounts, visit the Sorbonne, where she was teaching, and finish questioning Terrade's employer, colleagues, family, and friends."

"Okay for Théron," Nico said.

Indeed, he thought that Joël Théron's team would need all the help it could get to collect as much information as quickly as possible. Three of the four sections he managed worked on serious infractions—murders, kidnappings, missing persons, and sexual assault. The fourth dealt with counter-terrorism and had been particularly busy since September 11, 2001. The men assigned to it were worn out and constantly on call, just as he and his deputy chiefs were. He was already concerned about the holiday season. Right now, things were relatively calm as far as criminal cases were concerned. So Théron's men could work with Kriven's on the Jory case.

"I will deal with the paternity issue and contact Ms. Jory's gynecologist," Nico said. "Then I'll go to the Sorbonne. Go ahead with the rest. Use the usual methods. I have an appointment at eleven with the state prosecutor, so we'll do a first review of the investigation at ten. Let's get those scientists to move their asses on this."

Rost and Kriven left the office. Nico called Paul Terrade's sister. She answered after a single ring.

"How is your brother holding up?" Sirsky asked after identifying himself.

"He was up all night. He refuses to sleep. It's like he's keeping vigil for Marie-Hélène."

"He won't last long that way. You should take him to see a doctor. He has experienced a shock that he may have trouble handling on his own."

"That's exactly what I was going to suggest today. But Paul can be so stubborn."

Nico had the impression that Paul Terrade was in good hands. His sister was obviously sad, but she was dealing with the situation.

"I need to see your brother. It's urgent."

"Why? Do you have something new?" she asked.

"In a way. Can you manage to be in my office at nine?"

"So it is important. Of course, we'll be there."

"See you then," Nico concluded.

He then took the list of the couple's doctors, including their general practitioner, his ophthalmologist, a dentist, and her gynecologist. He was most interested in talking with the gynecologist, whose offices were certainly not open yet. He asked his staff to find the physician's home phone number, and he called it. A woman answered. He gave his name, and she got her husband, Dr. Jacques Taland.

"What can I do for you, Inspector?" he asked, sounding anxious.

"It is about one of your patients."

"Oh." He sounded relieved.

"Marie-Hélène Jory."

"I saw her last Friday."

"Ms. Jory is dead, Doctor."

Silence settled.

"She was murdered," Nico added.

"That's horrible! How can I help?"

"I need you to send me her medical file. It's urgent."

"I suppose that under these circumstances medical privilege does not apply?"

"Send me the papers today, and I'll send you an order from the public prosecutor. How's that?"

"I trust you. That's terrible. I told her she was pregnant. She was beaming. It's hard to forget that look, even though I deliver this kind of news all the time. Her blood tests should be in soon."

"In addition, I need you to make a statement. When can you stop in?"

"I'll bring the file over myself, say around one this afternoon. Does that work?"

"Perfect. I'll be waiting for you at 36 Quai des Orfèvres."

He hung up and called the Sorbonne. He asked to speak to the dean, a woman named Françoise Pasquier.

"I thought you might contact me this morning," she said. She had an authoritative voice and didn't bother with unnecessary introductions.

"So you know why I am calling?"

"What do you think? When a professor misses all of her classes, I want to know why. I found out last night. We have her companion's cell phone number. I am so sorry for Marie-Hélène and her family. She was an excellent teacher. She knew her job inside out and was very attentive to her students."

That's what Nico liked in women, their ability to be attentive to those around them, both in their families and on the job. That and the fact that they killed a lot less frequently than men: women accounted for only ten to thirteen percent of all criminals worldwide. No testosterone, less uncontrolled sex drive and rape. No doubt about it, he preferred women.

"Did she have any conflicts with her colleagues? Any problems with the administration?"

"None at all. I can guarantee that," Françoise Pasquier answered. "But I understand that you want to check for yourself. I suppose you will be coming to see us?"

The dean was clearly a very capable and intelligent woman.

"This afternoon, around three."

"I'll be in my office."

They were ending their conversation with polite formalities when he was told that Terrade and his sister had arrived. He asked them to sit down in the two deep-brown leather armchairs facing his desk.

"Have you found anything?" Paul Terrade asked, clearly anxious.

"In effect. Your companion was pregnant."

The two visitors paled at the news. Nico let the heavy silence last, even though he knew it was a questionable tactic, considering the circumstances. Terrade's sister placed a hand on her brother's shoulder, and Nico noted that her fingers were white from the pressure she was applying. He could hear Terrade's breathing, which was full of emotion. Was he acting? That was hard to believe.

"Pregnant?" Terrade said with some difficulty.

"About a month along. Didn't you know?"

"No, Marie-Hélène stopped taking the pill three months ago."

"Ms. Jory found out on Friday. Four days ago."

In a stupor, he asked, "Why didn't she tell me?"

"You had a busy weekend," his sister said. "A woman likes to choose the right moment, that special time, to announce something so important. I'm sure she was preparing to tell you, Paul."

Terrade collapsed. "My baby," he sobbed and groaned. The loss was adding to his torment.

"I'm sorry, but I am required to take your DNA, Mr. Terrade. I have to make sure that you are the father."

The man shot him a look. Nico knew he was being cruel.

"It's a routine test," Nico added apologetically. "I will ask a nurse to come by. In the meantime, would you like coffee?"

Nico called a colleague to escort Terrade and his sister to another office to handle the rest. All they needed was a hair, a few skin cells, or a drop of blood or saliva. The sample would be sealed and taken to the next high-speed train to Nantes. Nico disagreed with his superiors about DNA testing and trusted the Nantes University Hospital more than the Paris police forensics lab. He would have the results in less than twenty-four hours.

He wasn't alone very long. A section chief arrived without any ceremony.

"Want to know the latest?" the strapping man said. "The Élysée just called. The president's chief of staff wants an update on the investigation of Madame de Vallois's murder."

The Vallois family was well known in France. Delphine de Vallois, once a friend of the president, had been murdered two years earlier in her seedy eighth-arrondissement apartment. She had squandered her fortune and no longer kept respectable company. They had never caught the murderer, although La Crim' did have some clues as to who it was. They presumed it was a spurned lover. The number of bruises on the victim's body suggested an intense struggle. But they never had enough evidence to make an arrest.

"You know what I think of that case?" Nico said. "Send them the same report we did last time. They keep hounding us about this. We don't take orders from the Élysée."

The case was not *that* interesting, and they would end up catching the culprit. The division had time to work its cases, and this was one of its great advantages. Some investigations took months, even years. Marie-Hélène Jory's case was different. They had to act quickly.

"You said it, boss. They are starting to get on my nerves," the subordinate said. "So, it looks like there's no meeting this morning?"

At about nine-thirty every morning, the section heads would get together in Nico's office for a quick review of ongoing cases. Although they allowed themselves a cup of coffee, they never sat down for this meeting.

"No, not today. The Jory case has priority."

"Lucky you. I wish I were in on it."

Nico smiled. His teams loved their work. They all volunteered whenever an investigation showed signs of being particularly difficult. They wanted to participate and show what they were made of. It took a special kind of person, a meticulous intellectual, to be part of La Crim'. They were all experienced officers he had hand-picked for their respective skills.

The head of counter-terrorism arrived, and a morning meeting wound up taking place anyway. The international situation required him to work closely with all those involved.

"Here is the file on Chechen movements in France that you wanted," the deputy chief said. "Religion is not the only factor. Tribal relations play an important role in their organization. We're keeping a constant watch on their leader. I can even tell you when he takes a piss."

"Good. We need to tighten the net. We can't let down our guard. It could be dangerous."

"Maximum pressure. The men are on it."

"Perfect. That's exactly what the interior minister will want to know. And what about Iraq?" Nico asked. Well before the media broadcast the threat, and the world's leaders took a stand for or firmly against the war, his team had been placing daily bets, not on its probability, but rather on the date that it would break out. The ultra-confidential information he had in hand left little doubt. There were already skirmishes affecting the coalition, and the risk of terrorism had risen in France.

"Bombing victims continue to pile up over there," said the head of counter-terrorism. "We have to stay alert."

Nico nodded. What was the Marie-Hélène Jory case in the midst of all that? It certainly put the murder in a different perspective—but only for a moment or two.

5

ANNE OR CHLOÉ

Anne Recordon and Chloé Bartes had known each other since primary school. Now in their thirties, they were best friends. In fact, they were as close as sisters.

That morning, they walked together to the gym. They wanted to stay in shape and did what was necessary, exercising, eating right, and avoiding alcohol and cigarettes. These were the rules of their everyday life. They had attentive husbands and were successful. They were certainly happy, and their conversations often ended in laughter. Nothing and nobody could shake the ground they stood on and make them doubt the world around them. Absolutely nobody.

Except him. He had been spying on them tirelessly. He was capable of anything, even the worst. He had been following them since they had left home, as he had done for several days. He was determined and knew the tiniest details of their schedules, the routes they took, and the transportation they chose. Their routines were as predictable as a page of memorized sheet music. Even when they went for a walk, they stayed in the same neighborhood and shopped at the same stores. Sometimes a man let out an admiring whistle, which caused them to break out in laughter, like two shy little girls. But they had not noticed him. He observed them with a detached eye that registered each one of their habits. He remained invisible to them. He, who was nobody in their lives, had the power to determine their death.

§ § §

Nico leaned over his keyboard and opened his e-mail. Professor Armelle Vilars had sent him the autopsy report. He looked over it quickly. The tox screen and blood tests were normal. There was a detailed description of the knife. The criminal had used a whip first and then a scalpel to cut off her breasts. What was going on in the mind of a man who could do this kind of thing? There was perversity in how he tortured the woman, and the violence supplanted the meticulous organization. Nico knew that the nature of the murder and the way it had been laid out were clues to comprehending the culprit's personality.

Did he know Marie-Hélène Jory? How did he choose the victim? There were so many questions. The woman's pregnancy was confirmed. The embryo was described as attached to the uterine wall, the tissues just barely differentiated; the heart was forming, and it measured 0.4 millimeter.

Nico called his secretary and asked her to contact Dominique Kreiss. He wanted her to join the meeting that would take place any minute. He wanted to compare his analysis of the evidence with the psychologist's.

It was ten, and the entire team joined him in his office. Deputy Chief Jean-Marie Rost handed him a preliminary report. Nico acknowledged it with a nod. He knew Rost had worked hard to produce it so quickly.

"The couple's bank accounts are clean," Rost said. "There's nothing to note. The doctors didn't mention any health issues. One of our men is at the bank where Terrade works. He called about twenty minutes ago to say that he didn't think he was going to come up with anything significant. Terrade is a model manager. Ordinary. We'll know more at the end of the morning."

This confirmed Nico's hunch that they weren't going to make any major discoveries in this line of investigation. The answers to their questions were not going to come from the victim's side of things. Had she been chosen by chance? There was nothing to confirm that hypothesis either.

"What about the neighbors?" Nico asked.

"The guys were back there bright and early," Kriven said. "For now, there's nothing more than what we had last night. Jack shit. The hours fly by, and we're getting nothing new."

A lack of witnesses was nothing new these days, Nico thought. People didn't pay much attention to what was going on around them anymore. They were too preoccupied with their work, their families, and their television shows. Things had certainly changed in the past twenty years. Was the twenty-first century going to be the century of indifference, giving criminals more space to maneuver? He turned to Dominique Kreiss, who hadn't missed any of the conversation.

"Why her? That is a key question," she began. "The choice of victim is never innocent. The apartment was clean, orderly, and tastefully decorated. That shows a structured personality. Either she knew the killer, or he inspired such trust that she invited him into her home, in which case we are dealing with a manipulator. I see him as a sadistic psychopath who prepares his crime methodically. He chose his victim for her specific profile and left nothing to chance. He undoubtedly feels no remorse. He is intelligent and has a comfortable life. He is a man who gives the impression of being perfectly normal. I have not yet used the term serial killer, but there is evidence he leans in that direction. It's indicated by his use of a whip, which could characterize a fetish, and the mutilation of the victim's breasts. Both are elements that could be linked to the subject's relationship with his mother, just like the stab wound in the abdomen. These could be explained by some heart-felt childhood humiliation."

"Things always get more complicated with you," Nico noted, impressed with her analysis. "And what do you think about the murder scene?"

"A calculating murderer often ties up and tortures his victim. It is an expression of a desire for power and domination and an act of revenge for something in the past."

"But we are not there yet," Nico said.

There was not, in fact, any proof for what the shrink was saying. However, it was disquieting. And the more the investigation advanced, the more Marie-Hélène Jory's friends and family seemed cleared.

"I'm going to see the prosecutor," Nico said. "Then I've got an appointment with Jory's gynecologist, and I have to go off to the Sorbonne. That's my schedule. You can reach me through Acropol at any time. Let's meet here at six. Find me something we can run with."

Acropol was an encrypted and highly secure radio communications system. The device was bulkier and heavier than a cell phone, but it was confidential and quick. And Nico was sure to find one of his team members at the other end. He picked up the box on the corner of his desk and left the division offices. On the way, a travel agency caught his attention. Its name, written in white letters, stood out on a background the color of the South Seas, giving him a sudden desire to get away. To fly to the other side of the world, to forget his duties, to lie on white sand beaches and swim in warm, clear waters, to take the time to live—what a fine dream to share with a woman. Dr. Dalry came to mind. Clearly, he couldn't stop thinking about her. Perhaps he was just affection-deprived.

He headed toward the government administrative building, just a few yards away from La Crim'. He took in Notre Dame's gothic architecture just a little farther along the way. The spirit of Quasimodo and the monstrous gargoyles of the Galerie des Chimères—remnants of nineteenth-century romanticism—brought him back to his childhood dreams, peopled with legendary landscapes and fantastic adventures. But he didn't have the time or the heart to let his mind wander. The prefect was waiting for him.

§ § §

The Marais held part of the city's magic, with its private townhouses lining narrow streets between the Rue du Temple and the Rue des Archives. The neighborhood formed a triangle, with the Hôtel de Ville, the Place de la Bastille, and the Place de la République at its points. It was the preserved heart of the capital. A long history and well-preserved heritage let the mind imagine unbelievable treasures it once held and scenes with kings and courtesans that those stones had witnessed. He liked this enigmatic atmosphere. It was, after all, in the tower of the Temple Fortress that King Louis XVI had been imprisoned before being taken to the guillotine. It was also where the young King Louis XVII was killed under lesser-known circumstances. This was a neighborhood predestined for his crime. He was bloodthirsty; the right moment was approaching. He watched them. They were admiring the windows of the curio and fashion shops that had multiplied in the area. They had been dealt a good hand: they were beautiful and classy. But he hated their arrogance. They left a shop on the Rue Vieille du Temple and walked along the Hôtel Amelot de Bisseuil, with its magnificent sculpted gate representing the Roman wolf nursing Remus and Romulus. They were not far from home. He felt excitement invade him—nothing he couldn't control. Finally, they separated, one going to cook for her husband, who came home for lunch every day, and the other returning to her place on the Rue de Turenne.

She was the one he would follow. She tapped on the keyboard and pushed the door to enter the building. He knew the code by heart. He waited a moment and then went over the threshold in turn. Easy. He climbed three flights of heavily carpeted stairs, a sign of the apartment complex's prestige. When he arrived at his destination, he stopped in front of the solid door with imposing security locks. He was focused, savoring the present, the moment right before the appointment he had arranged for his victim. Then he raised a determined hand and rang the bell.

"Who is it?" a woman called out from the other side of the door.

"The mailman, Ma'am. I have a package for you. I need a signature."

She opened the door without hesitating. He presented the package, along with a more than charming smile.

"I'm sorry. I forgot my pen," he said.

"Don't move. I'll go get one."

She walked away. He quietly entered the apartment. It was all going as planned. She was not far, in the hallway, leaning over a drawer in an antique dresser. She rummaged through it, looking for something to write with. He closed the door behind him, which made her jump. He was wearing the same reassuring smile as he moved toward her. Her pupils dilated slightly, a simple cerebral motor reflex. He smelled her sophisticated perfume. Her perfect body left him cold. In fact, he felt nothing but disgust for this woman. Then his smile suddenly came undone, and his features stiffened. She stepped back.

With a vengeful hand, he slapped her. She fell backward, letting out a scream. He pulled an ether-soaked cloth out of his jacket pocket and held it against the woman's mouth. She couldn't resist. He lay on top of her and held her down with his powerful muscles. Her eyes filled with terror. She tried kicking. She wanted to scream, but it was too late. Her eyelids closed under the effect of the drug, and she stopped moving. Now his prey was asleep. Calmly, he removed the equipment he needed from his backpack. He exchanged his leather gloves for latex. He locked the entrance door and took an instant to explore the apartment. The living room was perfect. He carried the inanimate body there, took off all of her clothes, and bound her wrists to the heavy table in the adjoining dining room. She was nude, lying on her back, with her arms raised. He grabbed duct tape from his bag and gagged her. The effect of the anesthesia would wear off soon, but she wouldn't be able to scream. Then he sat down next to his prey and waited for her to wake up. He stared at her with a relentless, empty look. He would do nothing to her until she regained consciousness. He wanted to see the panic deep in her eyes; he wanted to hear the moans of pain. He would act slowly, getting the most from every second. He would whip her skin into strips. Most important, he would cut off those round breasts that she was so proud of. And he had a little surprise for her.

§ § §

At one, Dr. Jacques Taland arrived for his appointment. Nico stood and shook his hand. The man was approaching sixty and had graying hair, a portly belly, and a jovial face. Nico smiled at the thought that the doctor's family-man looks most certainly inspired his patients' confidence.

"Thank you for coming in on such short notice," Nico began.

"Of course," the doctor answered. "I'm very upset about what happened to Ms. Jory. I brought you the blood tests from Saturday morning that confirm her pregnancy. There was no doubt. The tests show that everything was normal, for whatever good that does now. Here is her medical file. She stopped taking the pill three months ago. She came to see me beforehand to discuss it. She was so happy when I saw her on Friday. She had made an appointment a month from now for a checkup, although the pregnancy promised to be smooth."

"Have you known her for a long time? Did she talk to you about the father?"

"She has been a patient for three years. She was living with someone, according to the information she gave me. I had noted that he worked for a bank. She didn't tell me anything more. She was rather reserved, not the kind to tell everyone about her private life. And I don't tend to pry. I need to build trust with my patients. Some talk a lot, while others are more discreet, and I respect their wishes."

"Captain Pierre Vidal will take your statement. You can give him the documents."

"At your service."

She shivered and opened her eyes. First he saw incomprehension. Little by little, she recovered her lucidity. Then panic took hold, with a brutality he had not expected. She thrashed about frantically, pulling on her ropes, shaking her legs, attempting to cry out, only to have the scream silenced by the duct tape. For a long time he watched her without blinking, until she resigned herself, winded. It was clear what would happen. Tears started to roll down her cheeks, which were swollen from the effort. He smiled coldly.

"Bitch," he said in a tone that was nearly detached.

More tears came. He liked that. He dominated her. He possessed her. She was his. He could use her however he wanted. He had the power of life and death over her.

"You have everything you wanted," he said in the same calm voice. "Do you even realize how lucky you are? Did you savor it? Because today you will lose everything. Forever."

He leaned over his bag and picked up a whip with a heavy wooden handle.

"Thirty lashes. It's an anniversary for me."

The terror in the woman's eyes heightened her torturer's motivation. The first blow bruised her skin. On the second, she twisted desperately, trying to escape. Blood came with the third. She was hurting. God, he loved that!

§ § §

Nico speed-dialed his mother's number on his cell phone. Certainly she had been waiting for his call since his doctor's appointment. She already knew all the details, thanks to Tanya, but she would still hold it against him for not telling her in person. He loved her, and they had a close relationship. But sometimes he needed to distance himself. When he was little, she had been possessive and overly protective, almost cloying.

She answered. "Anya Sirsky." Her voice was deep and self-assured.

"It's me, Mom."

"It's about time! Would you be good enough to at least call me after your endoscopy tomorrow? Do I need to remind you that you are my son? I worry about you."

"There's nothing wrong with me, Mother."

"Are you totally sure about that? I know you're in pain, even if you won't admit it. A mother can feel things like that. You're too tired these days. You can't go on living like this. Tanya, Dimitri, and I are not enough. You need to start thinking about getting married again."

"You can't mail order a wife."

"Don't joke about it. How's Dimi doing?"

"You saw him on Sunday, Mom."

"Yes, but do you have any news?"

"He slept at my place last night," Nico admitted.

"Again? Clearly, Sylvie doesn't know what to do with that kid."

"Mother! I don't want to hear you talk about her that way. Dimitri splits his time between his two parents and will continue to do so."

"But he adores you."

"His mother adores him, too. Let's not complicate everything. They both have to make an effort to get along so that they don't have any regrets later. This is important for Dimitri. I won't ask him to choose sides, and you shouldn't either. We've talked about this a hundred times, and I won't change my mind. So don't go putting any ideas in my son's head."

"Don't be silly, Nico. Am I going to see you this weekend?"

"Of course. I've got to go. I've got more work than I know what to do with."

§ § §

Her skin was covered with lacerations. She was moaning in pain and couldn't stop crying. He felt a mild erection, but didn't betray the slightest emotion, which terrified his prey even more. He removed the scalpel from his bag. He slowly slid the blade along her neck, between her breasts, and down to her navel. He was enjoying every second spent in her company.

"I am going to cut off your breasts. Let me warn you. You will suffer."

She found the energy to struggle. Horror in her eyes, she shook her head as a plea. He sat down on her, forcing her to be still. He caressed her nipples with the cold blade. Then he cut into the skin. Leaving the blade deep inside, he skillfully detached the breast from the rest of her body. She fainted. He had expected that. It was too bad they couldn't hold out until the end, awake and lucid, conscious despite the atrocious pain he was inflicting. He did the same with the other breast. When he finished, he placed the breasts in a jar he had brought for this purpose. He got up and prepared to stab his victim. One blow, quick and clean, right into that perverted woman's abdomen. Finally, all he had to do was cover up the crime, leaving a scene that would cause the cops to doubt their ability to find the person who had mutilated and killed her. The thought was enough to make him gloat.

§ § §

It was three in the afternoon. The staff in the reception area explained how to get to Mrs. Pasquier's office. The illustrious dean of the Sorbonne was around fifty and inspired respect. Despite a rather slight build, she exuded energy and determination. She shook his hand firmly; she was probably used to doing battle with men. Nico could see in her eyes that she could judge a person in a glance. She asked him to sit down at a round table, where a young woman placed two cups of coffee and some cookies.

"I put together a list of professors at the university, along with their contact information," she said. "I underlined the ones Marie-Hélène was close to. In an institution like ours, many people don't know each other. I'm also giving you a list of her students. I already questioned some of them to find out if Marie-Hélène seemed to be troubled lately. She was always punctual, never missed a class, and taught with passion. She was pleasant to be around and cordial. Her colleagues and students admired her, as I did, for that matter."

"Thank you. My men will start making appointments with these people. We don't want to overlook any lead."

"Was her murder that brutal? I talked with her companion last night."

Nico did not sense any unhealthy curiosity, but rather a feeling of responsibility and a determination to know the truth in order to face it. He chose to be frank.

"Yes, she was whipped, mutilated, and stabbed. She must have suffered terribly. I must ask that you not say a word about the specifics."

Mrs. Pasquier did not betray any emotion, but she blinked several times. "Thank you for your trust. Do you think it was someone she knew?"

"It is too early to tell. Could she have gotten on a student's bad side, over an exam, for example?"

"I was expecting that question. Here are the names of the students who received the worst grades in Marie-Hélène's classes."

"Could any of her students have felt amorous toward her?"

"There are always students in love with their professors. You might remember a teacher for her perfume or her legs or, if it's a man, his biceps. It's common. Those who teach know it and set boundaries. That is part of the job. Dealing with young adults just barely out of adolescence isn't always easy. But I had not heard of anything related to Marie-Hélène, or at least nothing out of the ordinary."

"Okay. So you have nothing to tell me."

"Perhaps because the murder has no connection to the university. Believe me, if I had the slightest reason to believe that it did, I would be scouring this place for clues."

"I'm sure that is true. Thank you for seeing me. The coffee was excellent. That's rare in a public institution."

"I buy it myself. That's my secret. Don't hesitate to let me know if you need anything else. I'll give you my personal number."

Nico was almost sorry to leave. He liked this strong woman.

§ § §

Anne was worried. She kept calling and calling, but nobody answered. They had agreed to meet at three-thirty in front of Victor Hugo's house at the corner of the Place des Vosges. She felt a strange solitude in this setting that was so truly theatrical. She couldn't explain it, but she had a bad feeling. It was four. She decided to go to her friend's house. She walked quickly, nearly running to the building on the Rue de Turenne. She typed in the code and took the elevator to the fourth floor. She rushed to knock on the door. Nobody answered. What should she do? She would contact Greg. A secretary answered. Greg couldn't be reached at the moment. She nearly screamed that it was an emergency, scaring the secretary. A silence. Then Greg's tense voice. "Anne? What's going on?"

"I don't know. Chloé and I were going to meet, and she never showed up. It's been forty-five minutes. I'm in front of your door, but she's not answering. Something's not right."

"What do you mean something's not right?"

"You have to come and open the door, Greg."

"I'm in the middle of a meeting with one of my biggest customers. I can't—"

She hung up on him. He would come. She had scared him. She put her hand on the heavy door and closed her eyes. She said her friend's name over and over, like a prayer. "Chloé, Chloé, Chloé." A ball of anxiety spread from the middle of her belly through her entire body. She began to cry softly.

6

SEVEN DAYS, SEVEN WOMEN

Nico was staring the crime scene photos spread across his large desk. The layout of the living room, a close-up of the tied wrists, the victim's clothes carefully folded and placed on a leather chair, the mutilated body. There was obviously a message in the pictures. He focused on each one of them, forcing himself to memorize every detail. The murderer had brought his own material: rope, duct tape, gloves so he wouldn't leave any prints, a whip, a scalpel, and a dagger. This was proof that they were dealing with an organized, intelligent, and skilled killer, one who was much more dangerous than a psychotic maniac. The man had carried out what could be considered a ritual. The complexity of the scene and the risks the culprit took raised the hope of discovering some clue. Perhaps he could find it hiding in one of the photos.

It was nearly six when Deputy Chief Rost, Commanders Kriven and Théron, and Dominique Kreiss reported to his office.

"Let's go see Cohen," Nico said. "He wants an update."

They went down a flight of stairs. Walking past an open door, they could hear a voice over the hallway sounds.

"Rape? Right—she was asking for it, I tell you."

Nico felt rage overcome him, and he charged into the room. He saw a uniformed cop standing in front of two detectives from the division, and he knew who had been speaking. The detectives started when they saw their superior and quickly looked respectful. The officer, realizing that he had been overheard, looked sheepish.

"Damn it! In these offices, I never want to hear anyone say that a woman was asking for it!" Nico yelled. "You don't ask to be raped. Is that clear, Officer Asshole? I hope you understand what I'm saying, or you don't deserve to be on the police force."

Nico slammed the door behind him.

"Good for you," Dominique Kreiss said. "How many times have I tried to explain just that?"

Nico nodded, exasperated. He said nothing more and hurried to the deputy commissioner's office. With authority, the secretary told them to come in. She had been working for the deputy commissioner for so long, he joked that she knew him better than his own wife.

"So, gentlemen," their superior said. "Oh, excuse me, Ms. Kreiss! I sometimes forget you are a member of the lesser sex."

"I suppose I should take that as a compliment," the psychologist responded.

"My mistake. That will teach me to watch what I say to a shrink. All those macho habits—of which I disapprove—acquired over many years spent working with men don't just disappear with a snap of your fingers. Please accept my apologies, Mademoiselle Kreiss."

"Accepted."

Everyone knew that Cohen had chosen Dominique Kreiss himself.

"So?" he said.

"Nothing really major," Nico said. "A thirty-six-year-old woman, one month pregnant, assistant professor of history at the Sorbonne, murdered in her home, Place de la Contrescarpe in the Latin Quarter. The crime was meticulously staged, leaving no clues. No witnesses. She clearly did not meet him in the street when she ran her errands in the morning. I imagine that he knocked at the door and that she didn't hesitate to open it to him. The couple had no problems. Everything was smooth at the university. The bank where Paul Terrade works confirmed that he is a model manager. Nothing suspicious with the family or friends. We still have to question Marie-Hélène Jory's colleagues and students and to find out if Paul Terrade is actually the child's father."

"You went through the lab in Nantes again, Nico," Cohen noted. "One of these days, you're going to get a real dressing down for that. Need I remind you that we have our own forensics lab? There's no point sending saliva samples gallivanting across all of France."

"They process DNA faster and better in Nantes."

"You're impossible, Nico!"

"I'm right, and you know it. We'll have the results tomorrow at noon. Just one thing, though."

"Yes?" Cohen asked.

Nico pulled out a picture of Marie-Hélène Jory's tied-up wrists.

"The rope is certainly some kind of boating material. Let's come up with a list of specialty stores that supply it and visit those shops. There can't be that many in Paris. We are still waiting for the forensics report, but I'm sure this is a special kind of rope that you can't find everywhere. We need to get a specialist to look at it."

"Good idea," Cohen said.

His secretary burst in, interrupting the discussion.

"There's a call for Chief Sirsky. It's urgent."

Cohen handed him the phone.

"Hello. Chief Sirsky of the Brigade Criminelle."

"Chief, this is Lieutenant Schreiber. This afternoon, my station received your fax about the crime at the Place de la Contrescarpe and your order to be immediately informed of anything similar. I have something for you.

I'm at 33 Rue de Turenne. I think you should get over here right away."

"Is it a murder?"

"Yes, a Caucasian woman, thirty-one years old, named Chloé Bartes, married, no children. She had a date with her best friend. Her friend got worried when she didn't show up, and she called the husband. At four-twenty, the two of them discovered the body and called the police. I have been at the scene for thirty minutes, and I thought we should alert you."

"Have you cleared the scene?"

"Of course, sir. The husband and friend are in the kitchen with one of our officers and two paramedics from emergency services. I had to call them. The friend was in shock and was having trouble breathing. My men are checking the building and keeping anyone from going in or out. They have cordoned off the apartment."

"I'll be right there." Nico hung up and looked at his colleagues.

"There's been a murder, Rue de Turenne. Right around the corner, damn it! Théron, you handle Ms. Jory's colleagues and students and the rope. Kriven, take your team to the Rue de Turenne. Rost and Kreiss, follow me. What do you think, Michel?"

"I'm coming with you."

The building at 33 Rue de Turenne was off limits to the public. Michel Cohen and his team lashed their badges and the officers guarding the entrance let them through with deference.

"There's a code," Nico noted. "Two possibilities. Either the murderer knew it, or someone let him in. It's a very upscale building. Chloé Bartes was well off. Kriven, get some men canvassing the neighbors."

Commander Kriven left the group to get the order out. The rest of the troop continued on to Chloé Bartes's apartment. An officer was watching the door. He called Schreiber, who showed up immediately. He was about thirty years old and had a dark complexion and raven-colored hair. He looked like a nice guy.

"Chief Sirsky?" he asked.

"That's me," Nico answered, introducing the others.

The presence of the deputy commissioner clearly impressed Schreiber. "It's not pretty in there," the lieutenant explained. "The husband and the girlfriend walked all over the scene and touched the victim over and over again before the police intervened. I did the best I could."

"You had excellent reflexes, Lieutenant Schreiber," Cohen said.

The man blushed a little. Led by the lieutenant, Nico went into the apartment. In the entrance hall, there was a dresser with the top drawer still open.

"Was it like that when you arrived?" Nico asked, pointing to the early nineteenth-century mahogany piece.

"Yes," Schreiber answered. "The bedrooms are on the right. To the left, you have the kitchen and the living room. Do you want to start with the victim?"

"Yes," Nico responded.

They walked past the kitchen and pretended to ignore the scene playing out inside. Chloé Bartes's friend was lying on a stretcher, with a paramedic on either side of her, busy with an oxygen mask and medical equipment. A police officer was supporting the husband, who could barely stand. He was in a state of shock. They went into the living room. An oak parquet floor and immaculate white walls highlighted a vast and magnificent living space that displayed a pronounced taste for contemporary art. Italian sofas, varnished furniture, elegant rugs, and modern paintings all reeked of the occupants' affluence. An oval frosted-glass table could seat at least twelve guests. The couple liked to entertain.

The victim was lying there, nude, stretched out on her back, in a position identical to Marie-Hélène Jory's. It was now clear that the case was taking on another dimension. Her arms were raised above her, and her wrists were tied to the table. Nico and Dominique Kreiss knelt at the same time, as if by habit, to get a better understanding of the crime scene. The others stayed at a distance. Nobody said anything. They were numbed by the horror spread out in front of them.

"We have ourselves a serial killer," Nico finally said. "The ritual is comparable."

"The woman's clothes are folded up there," Dominique Kreiss said. "And did you see the shoes? They have been placed carefully under the chair. The murderer is a perfectionist. Everything has to be in order. That is part of the staging. I am sure that the guy is well groomed and always at his best. Everything must be impeccably arranged at his place."

"The victim was whipped and stabbed, just like Jory," Nico said. "The breasts were excised and then returned to her body."

Pierre Vidal, the third detective in Kriven's squad, had turned on his tape recorder and was recording the chief's comments.

"Death is not enough for serial killers," Ms. Kreiss said. "This kind of person is looking for some original way to cause suffering and does so with an imagination that would never occur to anyone else. He objectifies his prey. He doesn't feel any pity but does experience an imperious need to mutilate the victim. The breast amputation is a way of further dehumanizing her. That choice is a serious clue that again brings us to the mother image. The man certainly experienced a childhood trauma that is motivating his actions."

"Something's not right with the breasts," Nico said. "It's hard to tell, but the skin color is not the same. I don't know—they don't fit."

"Marie-Hélène Jory's breasts?" Cohen suggested.

"Possibly," Nico said. "The medical examiner can confirm. What does it mean?"

"The two women are similar, Chief, so he's after a certain type of woman," the psychologist said. "The memory of his mother at the same age? Some sort of humiliation she caused him that he's getting others to pay for? That's what this scene makes me think."

"If that's the case, the choice of victim is not linked to the attacker's family, social or professional ties," Nico said. "He is looking for a prey whose appearance reminds him of his mother, which makes this investigation particularly complex. The rope is similar to the rope used in the previous case."

The psychologist nodded before getting up and stretching her legs.

"Michel?" Nico asked.

"I don't see anything else," the deputy commissioner said.

"Vidal, you're on," Nico ordered. "Rost and Kriven, you question the witnesses and let them go. What do you say, Michel? Should we search the apartment?"

Pierre Vidal handed them some gloves, and everyone took to their tasks.

The atmosphere in the kitchen was truly unbearable.

"We gave the victim's friend an IV of Valium," one of the paramedics explained. "She's not really in any state to answer questions. The husband is not any better. He didn't want to take anything, but he is very weak. That's hardly surprising, considering. What do you want us to do?"

"Leave us alone with them for a few minutes. Then you can take them," Jean-Marie Rost answered. "They should probably spend the night in observation. Has somebody informed the friend's family? What is her name?"

"Anne Recordon," a uniformed officer said. "No, not yet."

"I saw a wedding ring on her finger. Call her husband," Rost ordered.

The paramedics and the police officer left the kitchen. Rost and Kriven found themselves alone with the husband and friend. Rost leaned toward the woman. Kriven offered the husband a chair.

"Mr. Gregory Bartes?" Kriven began, placing a hand on the husband's arm. "I am a commander with the Paris Criminal Investigation Division. What happened is—there are no words for it. My job is to make sure it doesn't happen again. Do you understand? I need your help. Anything you could tell me could be key to the investigation. Mr. Bartes?"

The man finally looked at the policeman. His features were totally distorted, and his eyes were expressionless. Kriven shivered.

"Mr. Bartes?" he tried again in a barely audible voice.

"I'm here, Commander." The husband's monotone answer was almost zombie-like. "Ask your questions, since that is your job. But I can already tell you that your chances of success are slim. I have nothing to tell you. Absolutely nothing. We led a perfectly normal life until today. I don't know what could have happened. I'm afraid I can't be much help to your investigation. Let's hope it's quick."

Kriven didn't like Gregory Bartes's condescending way of talking to him. "Even something small, Mr. Bartes. Try to remember any detail that didn't seem worth noticing but could be meaningful today. Did your wife mention anything unusual happening recently?"

"No, I told you already. I have nothing to tell you."

"I was sure," Anne Recordon cried out.

"What do you mean?" Rost asked, kneeling near the woman.

"I felt it. She didn't come to our meeting place, and I knew she was dead. I can't explain why."

"Did you have any particular reason to think that she was dead?" Jean-Marie Rost asked.

Tears were rolling down the woman's cheeks. She was whispering, and he had to lean in close to hear what she was saying. Her eyes were closed, her face swollen with grief, and she was having trouble breathing.

"No, just an instinct."

Nico Sirsky and Michel Cohen left the bedroom and went into the office. They examined all the papers they found, including bills, professional documents, and bank statements. Nico pushed open the bathroom door. He looked for the switch with his gloved hand. A Jacuzzi occupied a large part of the space. There were two long bathrobes, two sinks, and a large mirror.

"Look, Michel!" Nico called out.

There were words written in purple on the mirror.

"Lipstick?" Cohen asked.

Nico approached the mirror, being careful not to touch it. Blood or some other biological fluid could be infected, presenting a risk of AIDS or hepatitis. He had to be careful, even with protective gloves.

"Hmm. I think it's blood."

The two men stepped back to read the message left for them.

"Seven days, seven women," Nico finally said out loud.

They stared at the words.

WEDNESDAY

7

SLEEPLESS NIGHT

It was past midnight according to his watch. The pale light on his desk lit up the entire room, creating a strange atmosphere, somewhere between a dream and reality. He pressed his forehead against the cold glass window, and his eyes followed the Seine, an age-old witness to human history. But the images of the two murders occupied his mind, and the victims had become ghosts that would relentlessly pursue him until the truth came out.

So much had happened since they had discovered Chloé Bartes's body just a few hours earlier. The message for the investigators proved that the murderer wanted to communicate with the police and manipulate them. This suggested that he had an overdeveloped sense of self and a strong desire for recognition. That was not a good sign, and this person had no intention of stopping. They had to catch him to put an end to the savagery.

The murderer had announced a seven-day agenda. What leads did they have? Was there any connection between the victims? They needed to do a handwriting analysis. Only the killer could have written those bloody letters on the mirror. Nico immediately ordered a forensics specialist to examine the message. Marc Walberg was the best they had. He began by taking several pictures from various angles. He studied the scene for a long time, occasionally writing in a tiny notebook. A periodic frown caused his glasses to ride up his aquiline nose. Nico did not interrupt him, because nobody ever interrupted Marc Walberg. It was not that he was pretentious. He just expected others to let him do his work. Finally, he turned to Nico.

"First, the person who wrote this message knows precisely what he is doing," he said. "And he is left-handed."

He dropped this piece of information as if it were obvious. Nico cleared his throat. Marc liked to be urged on.

"Explain yourself."

"The killer formed the words in a single stroke, which means that he did not have to stop and think. The use of lower-case letters is a convincing argument that he did not consciously try to disguise his writing. There's no trembling, no lifting, no signs of stress."

"What can you tell from lifting?"

"The number of times the writer lifts his writing instrument reveals his determination and self-assurance or, conversely, his level of anxiety."

"And this person is left-handed?"

"Some left-handed people exaggerate the curve of their wrists and readjust their writing angle. One final point: it is difficult to determine if it is a man or a woman."

"What do you mean?"

"Women write rounder letters with less pressure, while men tend to have more angular writing. Here, we can't really differentiate."

"Oh. But it could still be a man?"

"Of course. It could also be the unconscious imitation of a close relative's writing, which, in that case, would be a woman. You do understand that this particular writing surface does not help me go much further. A study of writing on something that can be picked up and examined from different angles is more useful."

"Thank you, Marc."

"Just doing my job. As usual, keep me in the loop."

Nico had asked that the mirror be taken to the police forensics lab. He had then met at nine with Professor Vilars in the autopsy room. Neither was in the mood for the small talk that usually served to lighten the seriousness of an autopsy. They got to work immediately, showing determination tainted with a deep feeling of discomfort. In view of the victim's physical state, they both had the sense that they were dealing with something very evil.

"Your intuition was correct. The breasts belonged to the first victim," Armelle said. "It will be easy to confirm, but you can already take it for a fact. The suturing is well done, and the material used is professional. She was sewed up by someone who knew what he was doing."

"So he removed Marie-Hélène Jory's breasts to transplant them on Chloé Bartes," Nico said.

"And he kept Mrs. Bartes's breasts," the chief medical examiner continued. "If we follow your line of reasoning, it was in order to transplant them on his next victim."

"He is completely over the edge!"

"He staged the crime in the same way, with the young woman bound, gagged, whipped, mutilated, and stabbed. The vital organs were punctured, and this led to massive bleeding, followed by death. As in the first case, the murderer inflicted exactly thirty lashes with the whip."

"So nothing was left to chance."

"That seems to be the case."

"It's a clue. But what could it mean?"

"That, my friend, is your job. And I don't envy you. Now let's look at the knife. I am extracting it carefully from the victim's abdomen." Professor Vilars held the murder weapon in her gloved hand and carefully examined it. The blade was covered in blood. Her eyes stopped on a detail. "Look at that," she finally said. I think he left us a little gift."

Nico approached.

"Do you see that? On the blade. There is a lock of hair, carefully knotted, held on with a piece of tape."

"What do you think?"

"Nothing. I'm going to examine it. I'll keep you posted."

"Can you do it quickly?"

"Shit, Nico. Do you really think I'm going to go home for a long bath and bed? My night is ruined. I'm staying and will get to it right away. I suppose that you'll be up all night too."

"I'll have to be. You can reach me at the office if you want. I wonder if she was pregnant."

"I'll check."

Nico left feeling confident. Armelle had a reputation for being the best. He met Commander Joël Théron at 36 Quai des Orfèvres at around eleven. The two men climbed the four flights of stairs. There, Nico unlocked a box and took out a key to a small door that looked like it led to an attic. They ascended an extremely narrow stairwell with a ceiling so low Nico had to hunch over. They entered the evidence room. It was a tiny space with white tiles and fluorescent lights kept at a constant temperature and humidity level year-round. There were some gruesome things in that room, including a charred suitcase that had held the cut-off limbs of a young criminal's father. There were also bloody clothes, weapons, and glass recipients in various sizes that contained not-especially-engaging contents, such as blood, saliva, and sperm. Nico took the rope used in the second murder, removed a sample, and gave it to Théron.

"Make sure to compare the two knots, and we need to know if the ropes came from the same supplier."

Nico slipped out the window that led to the rooftop. He walked a few yards, breathing deeply. He looked over Paris. In the daytime, the view was exceptional. At this hour, the capital was wearing its stage costume of shining lights. It was magical. Théron had followed him, and the two policemen smiled at each other. Here, they stood at the summit of their turf. Neither Parisians nor tourists had access to this panorama.

They returned the way they came and walked down to Nico's office.

"So, as I was saying, interviews with Marie-Hélène Jory's colleagues and students didn't provide anything new," Théron said. "We're not finished yet, but I'm not very optimistic. Other than a few unpaid parking tickets, there's nothing on any of them."

"And the rope?"

"In Paris, there are seventy-two retailers specializing in nautical material and fifteen distribution networks. I stopped at La Flotte Française on the Boulevard de Charonne in the eleventh arrondissement. You were right. It's a square-line eight-strand braided rope. It is very flexible, not very voluminous and absorbs shocks well. It's a 4.9-millimeter, ACD 700 high-strength mooring line. The team got a list of Parisian customers. We are contacting them now. But anyone can go in, buy some rope and pay cash."

"Would our man have bought this kind of rope without knowing anything about boating?" Chief Sirsky was thinking out loud. "Could any of Jory's colleagues be on that customer list?"

"Do you take us for amateurs? Of course we checked that out. The answer is no. Nor were any of her students or any of the people who were close to her."

"That would have been too easy. Keep at it, and check the second sample. We did learn something though: we have something from a boat that you can't pick up just anywhere. It's a start, Joël."

Dominique Kreiss arrived at Nico's office. He offered her a seat and handed her a large cup of black coffee.

Her tired emerald-green eyes shone in the half-light. The thought that he preferred Dr. Dalry's dark, deep look crossed his mind. At the mere thought of the doctor, a warm sensation spread through his body.

"Studying the victims' profiles is just as interesting as drawing up a portrait of the killer," the young woman began. "They're a key aspect of the case and give us an idea of the killer's fantasies. Marie-Hélène Jory and Chloé Bartes were actually very similar. They were both about thirty, successful, and established. They were not the type to go off with someone they didn't know, although that could happen to anyone. Both were also pretty brunettes, average in height, and thin. Nothing was left to chance."

Footsteps echoed in the narrow hallway leading to Nico's office. Kriven entered. "The murder was committed in the middle of the day, and there are no witnesses!" he spit out.

"The time the crimes took place tells us a lot about the murderer," Dominique Kreiss said. "He can strike in the afternoon without raising any suspicions. His work hours allow for that."

"If he has a job," Nico said.

"We are dealing with an intelligent, smart person who organizes his crimes perfectly. He has the profile of a sociopath. Generally speaking, this kind of individual has a successful career. He is socially integrated and can simulate emotions that, in reality, he is incapable of feeling. As I already said, he manipulates and has a high opinion of himself. He never feels any remorse."

"I'm intrigued by his message 'seven days, seven women,'" Nico said. "It suggests that there is a beginning and an end. But serial killers generally can't stop once they've begun. They constantly seek pleasure through their crimes. They can't remove themselves from the world they create."

"That's not necessarily true," the psychologist responded. "A sociopath can take on a particular mission within a pre-determined time frame and then go on to commit other murders in another way. Furthermore, you know as well as I that the serial killer at least unconsciously wants to be caught and voluntarily leaves clues to help the investigation. And he has an overwhelming desire for recognition. He wants to be famous; that is an important part of his psychology. These seven days are perhaps just the beginning."

"Hmm."

"There's something else," Dominique continued. "The murderer's message appears to have a strong biblical connotation."

"Biblical?" Kriven asked. "That's all we need!"

"Genesis, Chapter One," Dominique responded. "God took six days to create the world and rested on the seventh. I have the feeling there is cynicism in the message. As if our man were defying God, and through him, all of us, by killing a seventh woman on the seventh day. I think he is Parisian, living and working in the capital. He is between twenty-five and forty and most certainly white. Curiously, serial killers are almost exclusively Caucasian, and they tend to commit crimes only in their own ethnic group. Our killer has a close connection to the profile of his victims, which would confirm the rule. That is all I can say for the moment."

"Very good. Now the two of you should go to bed," Nico said. "I want to see you first thing in the morning."

Kreiss and Kriven looked at their watches. It was past three in the morning.

"Go on," Nico ordered. "Catch some shut-eye, take a shower, and come back ready to go. I expect you to be back on the job at eight, and I won't have any pity on you. If the murderer holds to his word, we could find a third victim during the day. This may be your last time to sleep before the weekend."

"What about you?" Kriven asked.

"I give the orders around here, and I am not obliged to follow them. I'm waiting for a call from Professor Vilars. And Théron is supposed to send me some information from forensics. Get out of here, now!"

Nico didn't have to wait long. Armelle Vilars, a professional through and through, hadn't slacked off. She called him on his direct line.

"Still at work?" she began. "And to think that the public accuses us of having it easy."

Nico couldn't help but smile. She was always energetic and witty.

"I worked double time, and I don't have much to tell you," Armelle said. "The bastard is very up to date on our methods. I sent the hair to Dr. Tom Robin at the police forensics lab. I pulled him out of his bed especially for you. He is the best molecular biologist I know."

Nico took the information as a jab at his preference for the university hospital in Nantes. Armelle also thought the chief's obsession was ridiculous and wanted to get the message across tactfully.

"Give him twenty-four hours, and we'll know everything it can tell us," the medical examiner said. "But I kept the best for the last. Chloé Bartes was pregnant."

"Pregnant?"

"That's right. One month along, just like Marie-Hélène Jory."

"Do you think there could be some connection?"

"I'm not Miss Marple. You're the cop. But it is surprising, isn't it? It could mean that our man has access to the victims' confidential medical information. That might narrow the scope of the investigation."

"So maybe our man hates pretty young brunettes who have achieved something in life and are pregnant. How many women meet that description in all of Paris? Can you imagine?"

"Come on, Nico, a little optimism. You are the best detective out there. If anyone can catch this scumbag, it's you."

She hung up.

Three forty-five. Deputy Chief Rost arrived after working all night with Kriven's and Théron's squads. Rost had a real sense of duty, like all others in the division.

"I just went over things with Théron and Dr. Tom Robin from forensics," he said. "I'll start with the knots. According to Robin's team, they're called fisherman's knots.

"Fisherman's knots? What's that?"

"The two ends of a rope are joined in an overhand knot, which allows you to slip one end of the rope freely through the knot until you have enough length to tie another overhand knot next to the first. Then you pull the two knots together so that they hold.

"Sailors use it often. The murderer has mastered the technique, one not familiar to everyone. Dr. Robin called the knot romantic."

"He has a funny idea of romanticism," Nico said.

"That's what I think, too. Also, the person who tied the knots is left-handed, which was deduced from studying the direction the knots were made in. The same rope was used in both murders. Now we have proof that it is the same murderer. The samples have the same chemistry, size, and color. Tests are being done on the message written in blood on the bathroom mirror. The blood type and rhesus factor are those of the victim. Dr. Robin tried to isolate fingerprints in the blood, using Amido Black staining—the water-based option. You dip the specimen in, let it sit for five minutes, rinse, and you have your prints. Except here, there were no prints."

"That's too bad. Good try, though."

"As you say. Robin is doing the DNA analysis. We'll have the initial results in twenty-four hours. But let's not kid ourselves. It's the victim's blood. Furthermore, they examined the clothing in detail but came up with nothing. Finally, Professor Vilars sent the lock of hair found on the knife to Robin. DNA analysis is pending. We will also have those results in twenty-four hours."

"Is that all?"

"What do you mean is that all? Go ahead and say that to Tom Robin, doctor of biology, biochemistry, molecular biology, genetics, and forensic sciences."

"Yes, forensics, too."

"Isn't it mind-boggling what you can learn from collecting, preserving, and evaluating evidence?"

"Yes. We know our man is left-handed, an expert in nautical knots, perfectly integrated in society, has a poor mother image, and chooses young brunettes."

"My wife is blond. I'll be able to sleep tonight," Rost said.

He had wanted to make a joke, but underneath those words, Nico heard a grim reality, and he didn't know if he should be surprised by it or not.

"She's expecting our first child," Rost added in an almost apologetic tone.

8

FANTASIES

It was Jean-Baptiste Colbert, a minister under King Louis XIV, who first proposed an ambitious crime-prevention program and created the position of police lieutenant. The police established offices on the Quai des Orfèvres in 1792, during the Paris Commune. Number 36 came about later, in 1891, when the Brigade de Sûreté occupied the third floor. From the time of Eugène François Vidocq, named the first crime-detection chief in 1811, to the Brigades du Tigre a century later, history was peppered with famous criminal cases, extraordinary investigations, and emblematic figures—both criminal and cop. The address symbolized the epic story of the hard-working and smart people who dedicated their lives to solving crimes. Nico was keenly aware of his professional heritage. He felt a profound sense of responsibility to his predecessors. Whenever he left 36 Quai des Orfèvres, he saluted the bronze bust of Alphonse Bertillon, the father of anthropometry and mug shots, who served as head of the Criminal Identity Division at the end of the nineteenth century.

It was five in the morning when he pushed open the door of his apartment, and it was too late to go to bed. He decided to slip into sweats and go for a run. His running shoes pounded the Paris pavement for an hour and a half. He needed that, to feel his muscles heat up, to build up the pace until the movement became perfectly automatic, with long and fast strides, his heartbeat regular. He chased the investigation from his mind and concentrated on the physical exertion. Little by little, an image arose: Dr. Dalry's smile. He liked that woman, and he was definitely interested in her. He crossed the André Citroën Park to the Champ de Mars and ran to the École Militaire. Then he sped up. He arrived home, winded but relieved of the tension of the past few days, mentally ready for his appointment at Saint Antoine Hospital. After he took a shower, he got dressed, paying more attention than usual to his clothing. He smiled at himself in the mirror. There was no way Caroline Dalry could resist him. He holstered his gun, certainly with the idea of impressing her, and left home, nearly forgetting that he was on his way to get a not-very-pleasant medical exam.

§ § §

Sylvie Sirsky was sitting in front of her breakfast, letting dark thoughts chase away the tiny bit of good mood that she had left. She played with her pills for a while before taking them, as she did every morning. Her diagnosis of depression was not new. She did have a naturally morose personality, but she had crossed a worrisome threshold. She went to see a doctor when she started having suicidal thoughts. The costly but necessary therapy sessions were not enough to help her overcome the darkness. Whose fault was it? Her own? That was what her doctor wanted her to admit. He wanted her to take control of her life and find meaning in it. But she knew what the problem was, because it had a name: Nico. They had met when they were seventeen. She immediately fell in love with the handsome young man who seemed ignorant of his seductive power. His tenderness had driven her crazy. He was so different from the other boys she had known. All he had cared about was her well-being. When she announced that she was pregnant, he shouldered his responsibilities. But one question kept hounding her. Would he have married her if Dimitri hadn't arrived? The door to her son's room opened, and he appeared. He looked so much like his father, she was overwhelmed every time she looked at him. Tears glistened in her eyes. She had to pull through, at all cost.

The silence in her office was oppressive this morning. It was an attic room, and to get there, she had to climb staircases and pass through hallways, all in a sorry state. She was sitting in front of her modest workspace, looking toward a narrow window that had three safety bars across it. She had the creepy feeling of being in prison. She chose to turn in the other direction and look at the poster of *Men in Black*, those heroes who fought monsters from elsewhere.

Terrifying characters hadt filled her career. Psychology students often focused on the victims of crime, out of compassion or a desire to fight violence. From the start, she had chosen to study those who committed sexual crimes, and she did so with gusto, even asking to meet imprisoned murderers to get a deeper understanding of their psychology. She had been perfectly trained for the job, which involved participating in murder investigations and tracking psychopaths of all kinds. She remembered her first dead body. She couldn't eat meat for three days. She had gotten past that stage. She was hardened and had learned to create space between her private life and her job, to the point of never talking about her police work with her loved ones. Her partner was not supposed to ask questions. That was their rule, even if sometimes he had a hard time sticking to it.

They had met eight months earlier, over dinner at the home of mutual friends. His brooding good looks had an immediate impact on her, even though she was not usually easily influenced by first impressions. He had come on to her throughout the evening and had wound up in her bed that very night. She still had not tired of him, because their sex was never routine. She blushed at the memory of the short night they had just spent together. Rémi had been waiting up for her when she returned home in the wee hours of the morning, after working for Chief Sirsky. He had jumped all over her as soon as she had come in. They hadn't made it all the way to the bed. Dominique Kreiss had not slept at all.

§ § §

It was eight in the morning. A nurse met Nico in the examination room, which had an examining table, a screen, cabinets, and a sink. She told him to remove his jacket and tie. He also removed his gun. She asked him to lie down on his left side in a near-fetal position. Then she adjusted the table until he found himself at an odd angle.

"Perfect. Dr. Dalry will be here in about ten minutes," the woman said with an authority that left no room for arguing. "I'm going now. You're a big enough boy to wait for her alone, I suppose?"

She disappeared before he had an opportunity to respond. The minutes ticked by. Then he heard steps in the hallway and Caroline Dalry came in. She was more beautiful than he had remembered. He almost wished it weren't so. But there she was, calm and charming, with a gentle look in her eyes. She had a presence as she moved about the room, even if it was just to go to the sink and wash her hands. Then she sat down on a high stool next to him. The screen was in front of her. Again, he felt a wave of heat spread through his body.

"Hello, Mr. Sirsky. This test will take only ten minutes or so if you do not move and if you breathe properly. I am going to insert a fiberscope in your mouth and slide it down your esophagus all the way to the duodenum. It has a flexible sheath that protects the optic fibers, and it is about twenty-four inches long. With it, I will be able to explore your digestive tract and take some samples to see if the irritation is bacterial. You need to swallow hard to help the instrument get past your tonsils. It is important that you relax and breathe deeply, or else the test will be uncomfortable for both of us."

She smiled. He felt a twinge of anxiety.

"It is not very pleasant, and you could feel like you are suffocating. Don't worry. It's only a sensation. Do you have any questions before we begin?"

"No, I trust you fully."

"Very good. I need you to face me. Hold your head still, and look at me. Open your mouth, wide. First, the nurse will spray some anesthesia in your throat. It will feel similar to what you experience when you see the dentist. Your palate and the back of the throat will feel thick. Then she'll put a mouth guard in to protect your teeth."

The nurse accomplished her mission, and Dr. Dalry gently inserted the probe in his mouth. It was very unpleasant, but he strived to show flawless self-control. He looked at her without blinking, trying to make the most of every second in her presence, even in a situation that was hardly to his liking. The doctor's voice reassured him at regular intervals, as she told him how she was progressing and how well he was doing. Clearly, she was the best remedy for the stress of this procedure. Barely ten minutes later, as planned, the procedure was over. Nico was almost sorry about it.

"Your stomach is fine," the doctor announced. "As I suspected, there is a small infection in the duodenal mucous membrane. It is nothing we can't cure, but it was best to make sure."

"And what kind of merrymaking will the cure entail?" Nico asked, suddenly more relaxed.

"I'll give you a prescription. You'll take an antacid for three months. And you'll need to try some lifestyle changes, including more rest, relaxation, and a balanced diet."

"It is not really a good time for that."

"Oh. Is there a rise in crime?"

"You could say that."

"You can put on your jacket now and holster your gun again."

"And that's all?"

"What do you mean, that's all?"

"We're already finished? When do I see you again?"

"Make an appointment in two months."

"Two months!"

Dr. Dalry laughed.

"Most of the time, my patients are happy when I give them that news," she said. "It means that everything is fine, Mr. Sirsky. You should consider yourself lucky. As soon as I have the results of the biopsy, I'll let you know if we need to change anything in your treatment, but I doubt that will be the case."

"Ah, good. Um. Thanks."

Nico didn't know how to stretch the appointment out any longer. What could he say? That he found her exceedingly attractive and would like to see her in another context? She held out a hand, which he shook despite himself, reluctant to put an end to the time spent together. He left the examination room and felt a huge emptiness. As soon as he left, he turned around and went back. He crossed paths with the nurse who had been there earlier.

"Excuse me. Would you happen to know when Dr. Dalry finishes work today?"

She scrutinized him, looking surprised. "I can't give out that kind of information, sir."

Her tone did not encourage him to continue the conversation. But Nico decided to insist. He took out his badge. "Let me ask that question again," he said, sounding annoyed.

"Do you really think a doctor has any control over her hours? You've got some nerve. Dr. Dalry puts in long hours—that's when she's not on duty all night long."

Nico raised his hands, giving up, and left without saying another word.

Caroline Dalry attended patient after patient. Her life was in this hospital. She was talented, but she still had to prove that she could hold down her position as professor of medicine at a mere thirty-six years of age. She worked tirelessly, earning the respect of many jealous greenhorns. She had graduated from high school at fifteen and had gotten used to playing in the big leagues early on.

"Doctor? Caroline?"

Hearing someone calling her from the hallway, Caroline turned around. The on-duty nurse was running toward her.

"Your patient. You know, that police chief. He wanted to know what time you finish work tonight. He even showed me his badge to pull the information out of me! Of course, I explained that we don't have regular hours here. He left empty-handed. You were a hit, doctor," the nurse said with a wink. She turned and walked away.

Chief Sirsky. He is a bit of a looker, Caroline thought.

§ § §

Professor Armelle Vilars had not gone home all night. What good would it do? While she was sewing the second victim back up, she made the wise decision to catch up on her paperwork. Files to read and sign were piling up on her desk. She got down to it and worked until she heard the footsteps of a colleague. She looked up and rubbed her eyes. He came into her office with a steaming cup of coffee.

"This is for you, Madame la Directrice," he said, setting the coffee in front of her.

"That's nice. Thank you, Eric. I really need it."

"I suppose you spent the night here. Did you find anything interesting?"

"What do you mean?"

"Come on. Everyone knows that the serial killer's second victim was brought in last night. So?"

"I've nicknamed him the Paris Flogger. He gives thirty lashes, not one more, not one less. Then he stabs them. Cute, isn't it? He knows the techniques we use very well and, as a result, is incredibly careful."

"But the brilliant Professor Vilars and valiant Chief Sirsky will unmask him, won't they?"

"Don't be sarcastic with me, Dr. Fiori."

He winked at her and left. He was by nature cheeky, and on occasion she had to put him in his place. Some colleagues found that insolence in him attractive, but he didn't have the appeal of Chief Sirsky. Nico was of an entirely different caliber, but he wasn't available for any of them. He was looking for the ideal woman, the one he would fall madly in love with at first sight. He was a romantic, even if he wasn't entirely aware of it. She hoped that he would find his perfect match before it was too late. Because "too late" always happened sometime, as the corpses that piled up reminded her every day.

§ § §

It was nine-thirty in the morning and Cohen was facing him, a large cigar between his lips. Deputy Chief Rost, Commanders Kriven and Théron, and the psychologist, Dominique Kreiss, had taken spots around the table.

"Let's get straight to the point," said Cohen. "He's going to go at it again this afternoon. We are looking for a serial killer. Nobody goes home until we catch him. I hope you have some serious leads to follow."

"The rope and the sailor's knot," Nico said. "We have something there. The two victims were pregnant, which isn't a coincidence, either. We need to work on these two leads. We'll know tomorrow if there's anything we can learn from the lock of hair."

"And what about prevention?" Cohen continued. "Anyone have any ideas?"

Nico let out a loud sigh. "A press conference?"

"What would we say?" his superior officer asked. "That no well-off brunettes around the age of thirty and pregnant should open the door to anyone?"

"And why not?" Dominique said.

"We need to get that message out," Rost said. "So why not go to the media? In any case, there will be leaks in the next few hours. We won't be able to keep the reporters at bay for long. We might as well take the initiative and try to avoid the worst."

"The worst will happen, press conference or no press conference," Cohen shot back. "Don't delude yourselves. But I agree. Nico?"

"Yes?"

"The commissioner wants to see us at the end of the morning. The prefect and the prosecutor will be there. We'll decide then whether to call a press conference. In the meantime, outdo yourselves. I want hopeful news in the coming hours. Show me you are worthy of the division."

§ § §

There was no doubt about it. He was suffering withdrawal. He needed to kill; the gratification was so brief, he had to start over again, to attack another woman to fill the emptiness. Beating her until the blood rose, taking in her tears. It was only when he returned home that he allowed himself some pleasure. He was no idiot, and there was no way he would leave his DNA on the scene. He held back.

The next victim appeared a few yards in front of him. She was beautiful, with long brown hair, thin the way he liked them, the face of someone who was fulfilled, a smile on her lips and determination in her step. He would bring her down as low as you could go. She would feel so much pain, she would lose her mind. And she would have no answer to the question they all had to ask. "Why me?"

§ § §

Tonight, her husband would be home late. An exhausting two-day business trip would certainly have left him drained. She decided to prepare a little surprise to relax him. She knew what to do and planned a light dinner, a good wine, and some fancy lingerie. The works. And she had some great news to announce. It would make him deliriously happy. He'd been dreaming about it since they met.

9

REALITIES

The police commissioner was a woman. Nicole Monthalet was fifty-five years old, five feet six inches tall and had short blond hair and dark eyes. She wore a tailored light-gray suit. Two discreet pearl earrings highlighted her femininity. Only a wedding ring adorned her hand. Her movements had a natural authority, as did her voice. One had to admit that she was imposing. Rising through the ranks of the police was not easy, and being a woman certainly made that exercise more difficult. She clearly deserved her position and knew the workings and the pitfalls well—the violence in the field, the detective work, the command, and the administrative responsibility—having made her way through them successfully. Nico had little direct contact with her, but every time they met, he left feeling confident and enthusiastic.

He smiled to himself at the thought. During the few years he had lived with Sylvie, she had often talked about the feminine side of his personality. She said she didn't know of any other man as attuned to women as he was. He was sensitive to the aspirations and challenges women faced in a macho world. Sylvie even swore that he had a sixth sense for understanding women. That made her excessively jealous.

How could anyone not appreciate Nicole Monthalet? Nico had seen the resentment some of his colleagues had for the "commissioneress"—the envious expression they sometimes used, as if no woman had the ability to hold down this position. He presumed that she had fought hard to avoid the traps set by those idiots. That made him respect her even more, and he was proud to work under her.

The prefect and the prosecutor joined Nico and Rost in Nicole Monthalet's office. They were well dressed and had the self-assurance of people who had done well in their careers. A third man was with them. Nico recognized Alexandre Becker, the magistrate who had just been appointed to investigate the case. From now on, they would have to consult with him. Nico had worked with Becker before but didn't have an opinion of the man.

Nicole Monthalet took the lead. She opened the file that Michel Cohen had given her a few minutes earlier. Pictures of the two victims were right up front, and Nico took note of that real lack of tact. Not that Monthalet reacted, but Nico was certain that this was one of the tests she faced on a regular basis, a message that nobody would wear kid gloves with her just because she was a woman. Nico held it against Cohen for letting that slip through.

"Gentlemen, we are here to review a criminal case of an exceptional nature and make sure the investigation is headed in the right direction. Clearly, there is a serial killer wreaking terror in Paris, and his targets have the same profile."

With an abrupt gesture that was almost angry, she put the pictures in the middle of the table so that everyone could study them.

"The murderer acts in the beginning of the afternoon," she said. "He is between twenty-five and forty years old, Caucasian, left-handed, knows about sailing knots, and can sew a perfect skin suture. He is sociopathic, methodical, and organized. The number thirty has a special meaning for him, and that is how many times he whips each of his victims. He has a problem with his mother, so he amputates his victims' breasts. In addition, he stabs them in the abdomen. He's thumbing his nose at us, as evidenced by the message he left for us at Chloé Bartes's home. We think that he will commit a crime each day until Sunday. If I am to believe our detectives, a young women will be tortured and stabbed to death this very afternoon."

"How many men are on the case?" asked the prefect, Mrs. Monthalet's direct superior.

"Two squads, which means twelve officers led by their section head, Deputy Chief Rost, and Chief Sirsky, who are with us here," she answered. "Our psychologist is providing her insight. That's enough. Our other teams are busy elsewhere."

"And the criminal is totally unknown to the police?" the state prosecutor asked.

Nicole Monthalet shot him a smile full of disdain. "We have fingerprint and DNA databases, but we would need to have the criminal's in order to run them. And we're long overdue for a single database that can consolidate all of the information about homicides in our country. It would be a great help to our police officers."

"We know how interested you are in advancing the SALVAC project," the prefect said. "The interior minister was attentive to your input and has agreed to go forward with it. He is even talking about creating a special police unit."

Nicole Monthalet nodded, impatient to move on.

"But that is not why we are here right now," she said. "Mr. Sirsky, give us an overview of your investigation."

"Since this morning, we have been visiting all the shops in Paris that specialize in nautical equipment. We are also trying to find out more about how these victims, both of whom were pregnant, are related. We are waiting for the DNA analysis of the lock of hair the murderer left for us and the blood he wrote with. These leads are far from insignificant, and we are doing everything we can to follow them up."

"In the end, we don't have any other option but to wait for another murder, do we?" Judge Becker said.

"We are informing all the precincts in the capital so that our officers in the field can step up their vigilance," Nico said.

"Mr. Cohen suggested that we hold a press conference," Nicole Monthalet said. "Reporters are going to run with the murders in the next few hours. It is perhaps in our best interest to take the first step and issue a warning."

"Who will do it?" the prefect asked.

The question implied that they were all in agreement, but he would not be the one to take the initiative. The case was getting bigger, and it would serve to have a fall guy if any complications arose.

"Cohen will handle it," the commissioner decided.

"Good," said the prefect. "Judge Becker will work with your office, Madame. I'll alert the interior minister immediately."

The phone rang as soon as Nico returned to his office. He saw that it was his sister, Tanya. He hesitated to answer, because he had more urgent things to do, but he finally picked up the phone.

"So, your endoscopy?" she asked.

"I have a three-month treatment for a little inflammation. It's benign and nothing to worry about."

"Perfect. I'm glad to hear that. But be careful anyway. So, tell me, I'm also calling about that dinner invitation."

"I really don't have the time this week," he interrupted. "I have a tough investigation on my hands, and I've been working night and day."

"Even if Dr. Caroline Dalry is with us?"

Nico was speechless. How could that be?

"Well, don't you have anything to say? It's tonight at our place, between eight-thirty and nine. And Alexis wants to see you. It's important, but he didn't want to tell me what it was about."

A dinner with Caroline Dalry was tempting, even in the current situation.

"Okay. I'll do my best," he said.

"I knew it! You've taken a fancy to the beautiful Caroline."

"Don't be ridiculous."

"Could you finally be in love?"

"Don't fast forward things, Tanya. And don't let it slip out."

"He admits it! I also heard a little change in her voice when I mentioned that you would be the fourth guest. Great! See you tonight, big brother."

Nico gave a loud sigh. His sister read him like an open book, which wasn't always very comfortable. But he didn't have any time to think about it; there was an e-mail from the Nantes University Hospital waiting on his computer. Paul Terrade was the father of Marie-Hélène Jory's child, according to the paternity test. Human cells had forty-six chromosomes arranged in pairs, and each pair contained strands of DNA. A child would get twenty-three chromosomes from each parent, and this made it possible to prove paternity. But the result of the DNA test was not surprising. The mystery would not be solved in the victim's inner circle. It was far more complex and perverse.

§ § §

Florence was feeling mischievous. She carried a dark package tied with a bright blue ribbon. It contained a pale green silk chemise that matched the color of her eyes. She had even dared to buy herself a matching thong. She was sure they would have an effect on her husband. He liked showy lingerie. That would be enough to get him to forget the fatigue of the last few days of work. He would let go of his tension in her arms, because she knew what he needed. She had bought his favorite wine, a Sainte-Croix-du-Mont, which they would sip with foie gras canapés in the candlelight. The atmosphere would be romantic.

She approached their home on the Place des Petits Pères. There was a plaque on the freestone façade. She knew what it said by heart: "From 1941 to 1944, this building held the Office for Jewish Affairs, an instrument of the Vichy government's anti-Semitic policies. This plaque is dedicated to the memory of the Jewish victims of this policy." She was Jewish, and living in this very spot felt like a triumph in a way she couldn't exactly explain. She entered the code to get into the building. Their apartment was on the fifth floor and had a nice terrace. She never tired of admiring the Notre Dame des Victoires Church from it. She set down her shopping bags and put the white wine in the refrigerator to chill. She had plenty of time to pamper herself with a hot bath. She would do her legs, her makeup, and her nails. She would be perfect.

§ § §

The doorbell pulled her out of her daydreaming. The man who rang it liked this little square in the second arrondissement, particularly the basilica devoted to the Virgin Mary and the six-foot-high stone cross taking pride of place above it. This was the center of Paris, no more than a few yards from the Place des Victoires and the statue of King Louis XIV on his horse. He was going to find himself face-to-face with his victim, despite the activity in the neighborhood. He could take his time, and nobody would be worried. A shiver of pleasure ran up his spine at the thought of what was to come. Then he felt the unsparing, glacial hatred rising from deep inside his soul. He imagined the expression of terror, the suffering, the mutilation, and then the death that would come as deliverance. In the end, there would be the staging of the scene in the strange silence that followed the torment and the satisfaction of accomplishing a job with self-control and precision. She was going to answer the doorbell. There was a shadow behind the spyhole. The sound of the lock. A pretty brunette greeted him with a wide smile. Her last.

§ § §

Nico worked nonstop, getting minute-to-minute progress reports from his troops. Twelve men in the field, led by Deputy Chief Rost, were visiting every shop that sold boating equipment and rummaging into the lives of the Jory and Bartes women. The two women were compatible with the murderer's fantasies. They both were pregnant, and that was probably part of the pattern. The criminal therefore had access to this information. But they had different gynecologists and had not gone to the same lab for the beginning-of-pregnancy blood tests. Clearly, their respective lives did not cross anywhere.

Nico had to step into the killer's shoes. What senseless need was he trying to fulfill? The man hadn't become a killer in a day. His personality had developed over time from childhood. He certainly had experienced physical

or, at least, psychological torture. This appetite for killing, this desire for cruelty, this constant dissatisfaction
would end only on the day he was arrested and locked
up. To find a motive, Nico needed to understand how
that mind worked.

Nico had to abandon his painstaking work for the
press conference. Michel Cohen wanted him there.
Reporters from the papers and radio and television
stations were gathered. The news would spread to all
of France quickly. Cohen briefly presented the facts,
without too much detail, choosing his words carefully to
avoid causing panic. He delivered a specific message for
women in their thirties who resembled the two victims in
any way. When he finished, the questions shot out. Nico
answered them, and a few interviews were organized on
the side, mostly for radio reporters needing sound bites
away from the general hubbub. Nico and Cohen complied, remaining calm and professional. They wanted the
press on their side; it would be key to what followed.

§ § §

He was experiencing intense pleasure akin to orgasm.
He admired the scene for another minute, standing a few
feet from the lifeless body. He would leave the building
and return home. He would have sex with his wife. He
needed to relieve the tension. His desire would drive her
crazy with pleasure, as it did every other time. She would
think it was love. But he didn't care about her love. She
was nothing but an object he used to relieve his urges,
and that was the only reason she survived. And while he
was caressing her, he would be thinking about his last
victim, about every minute spent in her presence, about

the cruelty he had inflicted. One day, perhaps, he would also get rid of his spouse.

§ § §

None of the precincts had called. There was no third murder. Their watches showed eight o'clock, and the men looked tired. They had all prepared for the discovery of another body and the hard work that would follow. But nothing. Dead calm. The investigation advanced slowly, and the lack of evidence made it difficult. Could the murderer have folded his hand? Nobody believed that; it showed on their faces. So what was happening? Had the criminal experienced a setback that day? Nico tried to imagine the scenario: an unplanned meeting added to the murderer's schedule, his feverishness in not being able to let out his sadistic urges. In the meantime, Nico decided that he could spend some time at his sister's place. In any case, he needed a change of pace. What he wanted most of all was to be near Caroline Dalry.

It was nearly nine when he got there. He immediately noticed that his usually calm brother-in-law looked distraught. He had barely said hello when Alexis told him that he needed to talk to him about something urgent. Nico nodded, but the only thing he cared about was seeing Caroline. The rest could wait. Tanya hurried to him, with the amused look of an accomplice. She was beautiful. Her coloring and features were like Nico's. She never failed to grab men's attention with her long blond hair and magnificent blue eyes. When they were younger, he had often intervened when certain boys gave her too much attention. He had learned a lot from this masculine attitude toward women, an attitude he forbade himself, despite his unquestionable power of seduction.

Tanya kissed him affectionately on both cheeks and prodded him on with a smile.

"Cute, intelligent. She's a real catch," she whispered in his ear.

Caroline stood up from the sofa when he came in and held out her hand. He couldn't breathe. He felt weak, and nothing came out of his mouth. Good God, he found that woman attractive, and he wanted her! A smile was all he could manage. He saw nothing but her, standing there without her white lab coat. Her long, thin legs were partly hidden by a tight green knee-length skirt. She was wearing black shoes that matched her blouse. A discreet gold necklace hung around her neck, crossing veins he imagined pulsing under her skin. At that moment, he would have liked being a vampire, biting into her soft ivory skin with all his passion.

"Don't just stand there. Sit down," Tanya said. "Can I get you a drink?"

"No alcohol tonight. I have to go back to the office after dinner. Fruit juice is fine."

"Is it those murders in Paris?" Caroline asked. She had a charming voice. "I heard about it all afternoon at the hospital. You were on the news."

"That's right," Nico said, unable to take his eyes off the doctor. "Be careful."

"And what about me? Shouldn't I be careful?" Tanya interrupted.

"The murderer prefers brunettes," Nico said, taking in Caroline's perfume.

"Oh, I showed a picture of Dimitri to our guest before you arrived. I couldn't help myself," Tanya said. "I'm always amazed at how much you two look alike."

"Do you have children?" Nico asked abruptly.

"No. I have dedicated my life to medicine, studying for many years and fighting my way up the ranks."

"Let's be clear about things," Alexis said, finally showing some interest in the conversation, "Caroline is professor of medicine at the teaching hospital, which is quite exceptional at her age. But she has worked like a dog to get there. You're talking to a whiz kid, Nico."

"That's pretty much like Nico," Tanya added. "Chief of the Criminal Investigation Division at the age of thirty-eight. That's a record. It's even given him a stomach-ache! Well, apparently that's not so serious, which is all that counts."

"True enough," Caroline said. "But he needs to take care of himself."

"Yeah, right. The only solution is for someone else to take care of him. He does have people who care about him, but that is no replacement for…"

"Tanya!" Nico cut in. "Be quiet before you say something you'll regret."

The women started to laugh, while Alexis was looking worried again. In other circumstances, Nico would have been attentive to his brother-in-law, but Caroline was there, with her long, thin fingers on her crossed legs and black nylons that rustled whenever she made the slightest move. All of his senses were alive, and he was having a hard time following the conversation. They sat down at the table. His sister had put them next to each other. His leg brushed against hers, and she didn't move away. His heart was beating fast. Tanya kept smiling at him, a sign that she had intuited his feelings. He wondered how Caroline would react if he put his hand on her thigh. But he would never dare, even though the urge was devouring him, and he didn't know if he would be able to resist for long. He wanted to throw himself at her. He saw himself tearing off her clothes and kissing every inch of her body. He was astonished by the intensity of these feelings. Caroline put him in a state he had never experienced before, and he liked it.

It was eleven-thirty when his telephone rang. The serious tone in Deputy Chief Rost's voice alerted him immediately.

"Nico, our guy struck again this afternoon, but they only discovered the body an hour ago."

"Where are you?"

"At the scene. At 1 Place des Petits Pères, in the second arrondissement."

"I'll be right there."

"Nico!" Rost called out before his superior hung up.

"What? What is it?"

"You're not going to like what you find here."

What did Rost mean? He sounded both uncomfortable and worried.

"Go on. Tell me," Nico ordered.

"The murderer's got you in his books. He left a new message."

"Perfect. That will help us. And since he has decided to establish direct contact with us, I won't be surprised when he does it again."

"You don't understand. It's meant for you. Just for you."

Nico went quiet. He was having trouble understanding.

"He wrote your name, Nico. You're the one he's challenging."

Nico stood up from the table and went to get his jacket. The murderer had designated him as his contact person. What did that mean? Did they know each other? This kind of relationship between a criminal and a cop was rare. So why here? Why him? Everything he knew, both professionally and personally, came undone. His remaining certainties collapsed. Was this some kind of bad dream? Was he going to wake up and spend a normal day at 36 Quai des Orfèvres, put an end to the fight between his son and Sylvie, and regret that there was no Dr. Caroline Dalry? He turned to face her and looked deep into her eyes. She was there, very real. She already meant so much to him. Nothing else had any importance, nothing but her. He held out his hand. He had to touch her, to make sure she was not an illusion. He found her hand and gripped it clumsily.

"I have to leave now. But if I could call you—"

He could hardly recognize his own voice. It was nothing more than a murmur. He saw her blush ever so slightly. Her response was a smile, a smile like the sun lighting up the dark hours to come.

"I need to see you for a minute," his brother-in-law interrupted.

"Later, I have to go."

"You must stay for a minute." Alexis was nearly shouting, and he was trembling, to everyone's surprise. "Please, Nico. Please."

Nico recognized the pallor and the shadows under his eyes as signs of fear. He decided to give his brother-in-law a few minutes. They went to Alexis's medical office, which was on the ground floor of the building. He hadn't been there in a long time, because, in general, he tried to spend as little time in doctor's offices as possible. Dr. Perrin turned on his computer. He was sweaty and uneasy. Afraid. Nico looked around the office. His diplomas were hanging on the walls. There were also framed pictures and models of boats and shadow boxes containing fisherman's knots. He remembered that Alexis loved sailing.

"Do you know how to make a fisherman's knot?" Nico asked.

"Yes, of course," Alexis stammered. "All sailors do."

Nico had never seen him in such a state.

"Look," Alexis said.

Nico walked around the desk and looked at the computer screen that was the focus of Alexis's anxiety. He didn't understand right away.

"My computer files—all my medical files. Someone has hacked them. I don't understand. And my appointments! It's been a real mess since Monday. I don't know… I'm scared, Nico."

"Calm down, Alexis. Explain what happened."

"The woman, the first one, it was Marie-Hélène Jory, wasn't it?"

Nico didn't answer. Her name had not been given to the press.

"That's it, isn't it?" his brother-in-law insisted.

Now he was sweating profusely. He was clearly panicked.

"And the second? Chloé Bartes, right?" he said.

"How do you know that?" Nico asked, wanting to understand.

"It's there! In my computer! I don't know these women. They're not my patients. Someone added their files to my computer. I have their medical histories. I even know they were pregnant. And look, look, Nico. He wrote 'murdered' at the end of their files. Nico, I never saw them before, I swear. What's happening? And there are pictures. I almost threw up! They are tied up, their bodies covered in blood, knives planted in their abdomens. I saw everything!"

"Why didn't you call me?"

"I found one on Tuesday morning. I thought it was a bad joke. This morning, I found the file for Chloé Bartes. Then you were on television. I made the connection."

"And the third victim, who is she?" Nico asked.

"A third? I don't know. Wait a second."

Dr. Perrin opened his calendar, which surprised Nico. "Valérie Trajan."

Nico called Rost's cell phone. The deputy chief responded immediately.

"Can you give me the third victim's name?" Nico asked.

"Valérie Trajan. Why? Are you almost here?"

"I need fifteen minutes."

The situation was totally incongruous, and if he hadn't held Caroline's hand a few minutes earlier, he would have thought he was having a horrible nightmare.

"That's it," he said. "Do you have information on her?"

Alexis typed on the keyboard, and the information came up, along with the murderer's announcement and the pictures. Nico studied the scene.

"Can you print that all out?"

"Of course," Alexis said, his voice quivering.

"How much time do you need?"

"Do you want all three files with the photos?"

"Yes."

"Ten minutes."

"Okay. I'll let you do that. I need to go. I'm sending my men. Did you have an appointment with this Valérie Trajan?"

"Yes. I mean no. For the past three days, I've had nothing but no-shows. And each day, my first afternoon appointment has been with one of the women who wound up being murdered."

"If I understand correctly, you had an appointment with Marie-Hélène Jory at two in the afternoon on Monday, with Chloé Bartes yesterday, and with Valérie Trajan today?

"That's right. Except on Monday, the office opened at one in the afternoon. So Jory's appointment was at one."

Nico stared at his brother intently, looking for an explanation in his eyes. He had known this man for fifteen years and truly liked him. Alexis was his sister's husband, the father of two, a conscientious general practitioner who worked hard. He had a calm nature and was always affectionate with Tanya. His mother loved him, which was proof that he had passed many unbelievable tests. Dimitri liked him. So what was there? He knew how to tie fisherman's knots, the victims' medical files were saved on his computer, he had appointments with each one of them, and none of them had shown up. That wasn't much. Then, just as he was leaving, another question came to mind.

"Alexis, are you right- or left-handed?"

"Left-handed, why?"

THURSDAY

10

VALÉRIE

Nico fell into another world. The investigation was breaking into a multitude of puzzle pieces that he couldn't fit together. The criminal was talking to him, which didn't make any sense. Alexis's involvement would certainly worry his superiors. There had to be some explanation. And as if by chance, Caroline had entered his life at this moment, creating another disruption. If he were a believer, he might have seen the hand of God in that. Dominique Kreiss had mentioned the biblical connotation in the killer's first message. He arrived at the Place des Petits Pères. Flashing lights lit it up. A worrying silence reigned, as though out of respect for the victim's rest and the living's suffering. Rost greeted him, a bleak look on his face.

"The squads under Hureau, Kriven, and Théron are here," he said.

Each of the nine squads responsible for investigating violent personal crimes such as murder, rape, and assault were on twenty-four-hour duty every nine days. Kriven's detectives had been on call Monday and had responded to Marie-Hélène Jory's murder. From then on, they led the investigation. Tonight, it was Hureau's unit that took the call for Valérie Trajan's murder. Hureau immediately made the connection with the previous cases and rounded up his colleagues, as protocol required, staying on to help under the orders of Deputy Chief Rost.

"We've started questioning people in the building," Rost said. "An upstairs neighbor named Florence Glucksman discovered the body. Her husband was supposed to come back from a business trip around eleven tonight, and she had prepared a special night for him. Around ten-thirty she realized that she didn't have any candles. She went downstairs to borrow some from Valérie Trajan. The two couples knew each other and were friends. Valérie's husband was also supposed to come back from a business trip. Florence Glucksman knew that Valérie's husband hadn't gotten home yet, so she wasn't worried about interrupting anything. But when no one answered the door, Glucksman got worried and went to get the extra key she had for her friend's apartment—they each had one, just in case—and she discovered the body. Mr. Glucksman arrived half an hour ago, as planned. Mr. Trajan cannot be reached. He should be here any minute now. The body is in the same position as the previous ones, except that it is tied to the foot of the bed. I only gave it a quick look, since we wanted to wait for you. Other than Florence Glucksman, two officers from the precinct, Kriven, and me, nobody has gone into the apartment. I called Dominique Kreiss. I thought you might want her around. She is already here. I think that's all."

"Except for the message," Nico said.

Jean-Marie Rost looked defeated. "Yes, except the message," he finally said. "It's best that you see if for yourself."

"Very good, ask the precinct officers to take care of Trajan when he arrives. There is no need to let him up. Let's spare him the show. And send someone to Dr. Alexis Perrin's offices, on the Rue Soufflot in the fifth arrondissement. He's there now. There are files concerning the three victims to pick up."

Rost looked alarmed.

"We'll talk about it later, when it's calmer," Nico said. "And Alexis Perrin is my brother-in-law, so don't be too hard on him."

Rost was disconcerted. He nodded and went off to give the orders. He entered the building, where Kreiss, commanders Kriven and Théron, and Captain Vidal waited quietly. Rost joined them, and together they went up three flights to Valérie Trajan's apartment. They passed other officers knocking on doors and questioning residents. It felt like an active but silent anthill.

"Has somebody called Professor Vilars?" Nico asked.

"Not yet," Deputy Chief Rost said.

"Do it, so she can get to the morgue and be prepared. We need to waste as little time as possible," said Nico.

Vidal opened his case and handed gloves to everyone. He took out a number of sophisticated lamps—white light, ultraviolet, and infrared—to detect any trace evidence. The art lay in differentiating evidence that could be related to the investigation from the ordinary traces left by people who lived there. The quality of the lighting and the police officers' intuition played key roles in this exercise. They advanced from one room to the next. The bedroom was farthest from the entrance, and they were in a hurry to get there. They stopped in front of the door, because they had to preserve the carpet. The beige-colored fibers could hold some useful evidence, and the last thing they wanted to do was contaminate it. Only Vidal entered the room, carrying his vacuum, which he used to lift tiny difficult-to-detect deposits that the forensics lab would analyze later. When he finished, they approached the body. The scene was as unbearable as the previous ones. Valérie Trajan had experienced terror before dying. Her clothing was perfectly folded and placed on her bed. Her shoes were neatly arranged side by side.

"Look at the slippers, over there," Nico said, pointing.

They all turned.

"They are hers, lined up like the shoes," he said. "And look at the night table. What a mess. Things are tossed any old way, with books and magazines just dumped in piles. I bet that Valérie Trajan was not a particularly orderly person. She was not the one who placed the slippers that way. It was him. It annoyed him, and he had to arrange them as he usually did. Vidal, make sure you get those to the lab. He must have been careful when he touched them, but you never know."

Vidal used special tongs to pick the slippers up and slide them into a box designed for collecting and transporting evidence. Dominique Kreiss couldn't take her eyes off the victim. The murderer had reduced her to a pile of pulpy flesh.

Nico touched Kreiss's arm. "And the message?" he asked.

"Behind the door," Kriven answered.

"Show me."

Bloody, threatening letters were spread across the wall.

"Nico, I am shattering my enemies, and Sunday, you will not be able to rise!" Kriven read aloud. "He's provoking you."

"What does he mean by you will not be able to rise?" Kreiss asked. "Is he addressing the police chief? Or is this more personal?"

Nico stared at her, at a loss.

"You need to be careful," the psychologist said. "This is becoming a very dangerous game for you."

They squatted near the body, each studying it from head to toe.

"There is a little lock of hair, there, between the breasts," Théron said.

Vidal collected it. The hair was short and brown, like the previous trace. This guy was playing with them. Nico focused and carefully studied the victim, memorizing every detail.

"You must have made some mistake," he said, addressing the murderer. "There are no perfect crimes in this world. You couldn't help yourself; you had to touch those slippers. Your obsessions are getting the better of you and that's how we'll get you."

"We have four days counting today," Kriven interrupted, uncomfortable with the concerns expressed by the psychologist. "What do we do?"

"Keep questioning the neighbors, and search the apartment, all night if you need to," Nico answered. "Check the husbands' schedules. Vidal, get that trace evidence analyzed right away. Make sure our lab guys get the results to me at dawn. Wake up Dr. Tom Robin so he can work on the lock of hair. Rost, call Marc Walberg for me. He needs to compare this message with the previous one. I want to know if it's the same person who wrote it. That's not all."

Nico took out a printout from his jacket and turned it so everyone could see. Everyone recognized the room and Valérie Trajan's body.

"Dear God. Where did you get that picture?" Kriven asked.

Nico took a deep breath and then sighed.

"At Dr. Alexis Perrin's office, on the Rue Soufflot. He's a general practitioner. The victims' medical files are on his computer, along with confirmation of their pregnancies and pictures of the murder scenes."

"Are you saying that…" Théron said.

"No," Nico cut in. "He's not our man, but my brother-in-law. It's totally incomprehensible. He even had appointments with each one of these women, who, evidently, did not show up at his office. Since Monday, his appointments have been in shambles. Someone must be playing with his calendar and his computer."

"Why?" Rost asked. He understood the significance of this development.

"The killer really has something against Nico," Dominique Kreiss said. "To the point that he's involving a family member. It's very troubling."

"We can't eliminate this Perrin lead," Kriven said. "Isn't that right, Nico?"

"I know. You take care of it, David. Go there. Look into it closely. I didn't have time, and I'm certainly not the one to do it. Call in a computer specialist to look at Alexis's computer. We need to find out how the data got on it. Ask Bastien Gamby. He's the best."

The counter-terrorism section was composed of three six-person squads. It also had its own research department and a top-notch computer expert, Gamby.

"Are you thinking it's been hacked?" Kriven asked.

"I'm not thinking anything. I want to know. Check Dr. Perrin's appointments for the afternoon. Maybe the name of the next victim is on his calendar. And there's more. Alexis is left-handed and loves sailing. That means he knows about fisherman's knots, and some are even framed in his office."

"Shit!" Rost let slip.

"I don't understand," Nico said. "There are too many coincidences. I'm aware of that. But it is quite simply impossible. I've known Alexis for fifteen years. He doesn't have the profile of a murderer. For crying out loud, he's been sleeping with my sister all this time! Please, let's not jump to any conclusions. It's too serious."

"Especially if we are dealing with someone who is after you and knows how to make things hard for you," Dominique said.

"Why is he killing these women if he's after me?"

"These women are the focus of his fantasies," the psychologist said. "I have no doubt about that. But you are the person he has decided to challenge. Perhaps he knows you and hates you for what you represent, or he wants to drag you into his murderous rage."

"But what can I possible be to him?"

"You're head of France's elite crime division at the age of thirty-eight. You're on a roll. Maybe he wants you to pay for your success, simply because he's jealous. Or maybe it's someone you put away. There could be a thousand reasons. Think about your private life, as well."

Nico shrugged. His private life was pretty ordinary, with the exception of a ray of sunlight that had just appeared—Caroline Dalry. Sunlight so hot, so luminous that he was already afraid of losing it.

"Can you give me something in writing?" Nico asked the psychologist.

"I'll take care of it tonight."

"Perfect. I'm off to the autopsy. It is nearly two in morning. Let's meet at, say, five, in my office. Let Cohen know, along with the investigating magistrate."

Eric Fiori greeted him at the medical examiner's office. He looked furious, and Nico politely asked why, even though he had more pressing matters on his mind.

"I'm the one on duty tonight," Fiori said curtly.

Nico looked at him, not understanding.

"I could have handled the new victim myself. I'm qualified enough for that. But you preferred to call Professor Vilars."

"That's true," Nico said.

"I find that unacceptable. Do you know how long I've worked here?"

"That is not the issue. Okay, you're not happy. But Professor Vilars is the chief medical examiner, and you have to understand that for a case of this importance, I prefer to rely on her best judgment."

"I give up. But you know what I think. Follow me. Armelle is getting ready for the autopsy."

Nico complied, surprised by the doctor's attitude and the way he referred to his boss by her first name. It was probably a demonstration of some repressed machismo, a chafing against having to work under a woman, even a woman of Professor Vilars's caliber.

Armelle was setting up her instruments. When he entered, she gave him a womanly smile, both gentle and encouraging, which then disappeared behind the white mask she tied behind her neck. She put on a second pair of gloves for better protection. The investigating magistrate, Alexandre Becker, came in at that moment.

"You would have waited for me, I suppose?" he said.

"I am entirely at your disposal, *Monsieur le Juge*," Professor Vilars responded, with enough seriousness to avoid further criticism, but with a touch of sarcasm to show that she had not particularly appreciated the comment.

"Dr. Eric Fiori will assist me, since he is chomping at the bit," Armelle continued. "Let's begin, if you will."

She started by inspecting the body, describing what she was doing as she moved along.

"I count thirty lashes of the whip, as with the other victims. It is clearly not a coincidence. The breasts have been amputated and replaced with those of the previous victim, Chloé Bartes. There is a single stab wound to the abdomen. The knife shows the same characteristics as the previous ones. Forensics will confirm, providing additional proof that it is the same murderer."

Armelle had been at it for an hour already, and Nico would have preferred that it last only a few minutes. He glanced at the investigating magistrate, who remained silent, showing no emotion. The coroner made an incision in the victim and skillfully opened her up, examining each organ. There was a heavy silence in the room while she looked for early signs of pregnancy.

"Valérie Trajan was one month pregnant," Professor Vilars announced in a gloomy voice.

How was it possible? How did the murderer have this information? And what role did Alexis play in this ghoulish plan? These were the questions hounding Nico while Armelle continued the autopsy.

"Well, look at that."

"What is it?" Nico asked impatiently.

"Mrs. Trajan must have worn contact lenses. But there isn't one on her right eye. She must have lost it. I am extracting the one from the left eye. I will have the contact lens examined and a sample taken from its surface for genetic analysis."

"I'll confirm that she wore them," Nico said.

"We don't have much to work with," she concluded. "I will provide you with the time of death. Based on my initial observations, it happened at the beginning of the afternoon. I'm going to look more closely, and I will get my report to you in the morning, judge."

It was four in the morning. Nico agreed to meet with Becker an hour later at headquarters and hurried out of the medical examiner's office. He didn't really like the place and had much to do.

Nico had barely gotten into his car when he decided it was time to let Cohen know. He woke him up and started summarizing the night's events. He didn't usually provide him with all the details of an investigation, but Nico was now personally involved in this case, and he could not leave his superior in the dark. Cohen, too, decided to report to headquarters. Then Nico contacted Jean-Marie Rost, who was still at the murder scene with the division's teams.

"Marc Walberg is very absorbed in the killer's message," the deputy chief said. "You know him. We don't want to bother him. He promised to have some conclusions for our meeting at five. We searched the Trajan apartment from top to bottom. You were right. The victim was fairly disorderly. Her clothing was all over the closet, her underwear just thrown in the drawers. She wasn't the type of women to set out her slippers the way we found them. We'll have to see if that leads somewhere. Mr. Trajan arrived not long after you left. He is in shock. I sent him to the hospital. I'll question him a little later, and I'll call his place of employment when it opens."

"I'd like you to verify a little something for me," Nico said. "Check for any contact lenses in the bathroom or the bedroom. The victim should have worn them."

"I'll do that now. See you later."

They hung up. Nico arrived at 36 Quai des Orfèvres and immediately went to the division's offices. Nets were spread between the floors of the building, just in case someone was tempted to jump over the rails. There were showcases on each level with a large collection of medals and uniforms. The Criminal Police Benevolent Association also used the space to hang posters announcing Beaujolais Nouveau celebrations, the staff Christmas party, retiree dinners, and the like. Team solidarity showed whenever there was good reason, especially the death of a member of the service.

Nico took refuge in his office. His cell phone showed that his sister had tried to reach him several times during the night. He called her.

"Good God, Nico! What's happening? Alexis is in a terrible state, and two police officers are still with him in his office."

"I'm sorry, Tanya. I should have called you to explain, but I admit that I have not had a minute to myself. And the whole thing is very strange."

"What whole thing? Please, tell me."

"I'm working on the serial killer case. Alexis has confidential information about the victims."

There was silence.

"Tanya? Listen, Alexis doesn't understand what is going on, and neither do we. What we know for certain is that the criminal has decided to target me. I would not be surprised if he tried to involve my family members. We just have two or three small things to check."

"You don't have any doubts about Alexis, do you?"

"Of course not, but we need to find out who is manipulating us as quickly as possible. I have requested police protection for you. I recommend that you take time off from work until further notice. Don't let the kids go to school. Stay home for the time being."

"You're scaring me, Nico. Nothing like this has ever happened to us before."

"I know. I'm sorry, believe me."

"Promise me that you will find who is doing this."

"You're doubting me? Have I ever let you down?"

"Of course not."

"So give me a few days, and this thing will be over. I promise."

"What about Dimitri? And Mom? Are they in danger?"

Nico sighed. To tell the truth, he didn't have the slightest idea.

"Ask Maman to stay with you until Sunday. I won't be able to get enough backup to ensure your safety if you're spread out. I'll call Sylvie later."

"Okay. And if you need us to take Dimitri in, we can do it, no problem."

"Thank you. Did Caroline leave?"

"Right after you did. She isn't aware of anything. She only noticed that Alexis wasn't acting normal. I wouldn't be surprised if she calls today to make sure that everything is all right. What should I tell her?"

"I'll take care of it."

"I would have guessed as much. You're hot on her. You can tell a mile away."

"Tanya…"

"Don't deny it. You've got good taste. She's worth it, clearly. I'm sure she noticed that you're interested in her."

"How's that?"

"Nico, you were acting like a teenager. You were devouring her with your eyes. For a minute there, I thought you were going to jump all over her. Do you really think she didn't get it? Come on."

"Oh."

"Seize the day, Nico. I'll let you work. Keep me posted, please."

She ended the call. He had started thinking about Caroline again.

11

UNCERTAINTY

It was five in the morning. They had just sat down at the rectangular table in the office. Alexandre Becker was acting haughty. He was the boss and clearly wanted to mark his territory. Police officers were there to execute the magistrate's orders. They carried out their investigation-related duties only when authorized by a *commission rogatoire* mandate. It was up to the magistrate to give more or less independence to the police, as he saw fit. Nico did not like the man's sense of self-importance. But he refused to let his personal feelings come between the police and the justice system. He knew he had to keep them to himself.

"Let's get going and be practical," Becker said. "I suggest we review the investigation and set up a plan of action."

Everyone nodded.

"Deputy Chief Rost? Did you get anything from questioning the neighbors?"

"Zilch. The girl most probably opened the door to her murderer. There is no sign of breaking and entering, no suspicious noises in the building. Nobody saw or heard anything."

"What about the husband's schedule? And Glucksman's?" Nico asked.

"Trajan is in such a state of shock that we still haven't been able to question him," Joël Théron said. "He was taken to the hospital, where he is under police guard. I'll call his office in the morning. Glucksman is off the hook. We checked and confirmed that he was on a business trip. Two of his colleagues were with him all day. His wife has a shop, and she decided to take the day off."

"And Valérie Trajan?"

"She was a pharmacist and worked in a drugstore four days a week," Théron said. "She didn't work on Wednesdays, a habit she established with the expectation of having children."

Nico continued. "What did Walberg have to say about the killer's writing?"

"The two messages were written by the same person, who again seems to be left-handed," Rost said. "There is a notable difference. Now there are peaks, trembling, and a greater contact angle."

"Which means?" Cohen asked, impatient.

"The writing is less regular, showing more nervousness or excitement."

"I want Walberg to compare the writing with Dr. Alexis Perrin's," Nico ordered.

"I think that is an excellent idea," Cohen said.

"I'll take care of it," Rost added.

"And what about the Trajan apartment search?" Nico asked.

"Nothing," Rost said, disappointed. "All we got was confirmation that Valérie Trajan was somewhat disorderly by nature and that it is certainly the murderer who arranged the slippers, as you suggested right away. They are at the lab, along with her clothing and shoes. Oh, and I didn't find any contact lenses."

"That's impossible. Did you look everywhere?" Nico asked.

"In every corner. I understood that it was important. And Florence Glucksman said that Valérie Trajan never had any problems with her eyesight."

"That's odd. Professor Vilars found a contact lens on the victim's left eye."

"I may have the solution to this mystery," Kriven said. "The lab found a contact lens in the trace evidence that Vidal picked up with the vacuum. He called five minutes before the meeting to let me know. The lab is comparing the two, along with DNA from both of them."

"The most plausible explanation is that Valérie Trajan lost a contact when she was attacked," Nico suggested. "But why didn't we find other contacts in her home, and why did her friend say she had perfect vision? We need to ask her husband. Furthermore, a lock of blond hair was left for us between her breasts. The police forensics lab is examining it. In the morning, we'll have the first results concerning the brown hair we found on the knife used to kill Chloé Bartes. As for the blood used by the criminal to write the message, it is probably the victim's, but we have to check."

Nico paused. He did not want to monopolize the meeting or take the lead when that was, in theory, his boss's job or the investigating magistrate's.

"Has there been any progress on the rope and the fisherman's knot?" Alexandre Becker asked, showing that he was familiar with the case.

"The same batch of rope was used in the first two cases," Nico said. "The fisherman's knots were made by a left-handed person. Théron, do you have anything from the third case?"

"It's a lefty again and the same kind of knot. The rope is being tested."

"The victim's breasts were amputated and exchanged with those of Chloé Bartes," Nico said. "And, finally, the autopsy proved that Trajan was one month pregnant."

"How is that possible?" Judge Becker spoke up. "The killer obviously has access to confidential medical information. In any case, since they only recently got pregnant, that means that he chooses the victims not very long before committing the crime. He acts very quickly. But at the same time, he seems to know everything about the daily activities of the victims and the people close to them. Trajan didn't work that day, and he knew. And this Alexis Perrin? Is he our prime suspect?"

There was an awkward silence.

"Dr. Perrin is Chief Sirsky's brother-in-law," Cohen said. "It's a strange coincidence, particularly because the murderer decided to target Nico directly in the messages he is leaving. So let's slow down. The killer is surely setting a trap. Of course, that puts us in an uncomfortable position. For the time being, Nico stays on the investigation. He's the head of the division, and we need his experience. Furthermore, taking him off the case is what the killer wants."

Everyone turned to Judge Becker. The ball was in his court. He sighed.

"Fine. I'll tell the prosecutor what you have decided. Let's stop there for now. Chief Sirsky gets the benefit of the doubt. I know his ability to get the job done. But let it be understood, I reserve the right to remove him from the case at any time. Now, Mr. Sirsky, tell me about your brother-in-law's involvement in this thing."

Nico recounted the facts and mentioned that Bastien Gamby had joined the investigation.

"Bastien Gamby?" the investigating magistrate asked.

"The computer specialist from counter-terrorism," Nico answered. "Nobody's better. The section is really busy right now, but I thought the seriousness of our case called for Gamby's expertise. Do you have anything to add, Kriven?"

"I pulled Bastien from his bed, and he met me at Dr. Perrin's office. Here are his conclusions. Alexis Perrin has an Internet connection and is networked with an off-site secretarial service that manages his appointments. This is a frequent practice. A secretary is responsible for several doctors, answers their calls, and schedules appointments. This kind of network is easy to hack into, because users sometimes connect to specific sites, for example, a special medical site, and leave records of their computer addresses, which allow a hacker to break in and transfer whatever data or file he wants from the Internet or even from other members of the network."

"Do we know if his computer was hacked?" Becker cut in.

"No. Gamby installed remote monitoring software on Perrin's machine, and starting now, if someone tries to get onto his hard disk, we'll be able to trace him."

"So Dr. Perrin could very well have put together the medical files of the three victims?" Alexandre Becker insisted.

"There is nothing that confirms or disproves that hypothesis," Kriven admitted.

"Except that Alexis had not even seen them yet," Nico said. "To be sure, all you have to do is go back over his schedule. David, did you record how long it takes to get from his office to the victims' apartments? We know the time that Dr. Perrin had available, considering his cancelled appointments."

"I'm sorry, but that doesn't get your brother-in-law off the hook," Becker said. "He could have had enough time to bind and torture the victims, return to his office to see patients, and then go back to finish off the women. It's not out of the question. Also, he says he had other patients who didn't show for their appointments, and when we tried to check them out, we discovered that they don't exist. The names and addresses on his records are fake. Perrin could have invented them."

"Except that it was the secretary who took the calls," Kriven said abruptly, happy to add something in Nico's favor. "I checked. She is a gem and writes everything down, including the date and time of the calls, along with the patients' names."

"Could he have masked his voice and called the secretary himself?" the magistrate asked.

"Anything is possible," Cohen said. "But Nico answers for Perrin. Let's not go off chasing a bad lead. Remember that Nico is being targeted personally, as we saw clearly in the last message. Let's take a look at the people Nico has arrested for sex crimes—the ones who've served their time. Revenge could be enough reason to go after him."

"Of course, we do not want to neglect any lead," Magistrate Becker said. "However, I'd like to question Dr. Perrin."

"I took the initiative to put him and his family under police protection," Nico said.

"That's fine. You did the right thing," Cohen said.

"If I may," Kriven said, "the team has already found fake appointments on Dr. Perrin's schedule for the coming days."

"And who's scheduled for his first afternoon appointment today?" Nico asked, sounding worried.

"A woman," Kriven said.

"And do you know who it is? Did you contact her?"

"You're not going to like this, Nico."

"What's happening now?" Cohen asked, having a hard time hiding his impatience.

"At two today, Dr. Perrin is scheduled to see Sylvie Sirsky," Kriven said. "That's Nico's ex-wife. I called her, and she never made the appointment."

"Shit!" Nico yelled, slamming his fist on the table.

"Is she the murderer's type?" Becker asked.

"More or less."

"Get her under protection," the magistrate said.

Nico stared at him and saw some compassion in his eyes. He was surprised by the judge's reaction. Perhaps

Becker did have a sensitive side that he kept hidden. The man rose a little in his esteem.

"Judge Becker is right," Cohen said. "Get some officers to watch your ex and your son. The murderer really seems focused on you, but we still don't know why."

"We've got our work cut out for us. It's going to be a long day. Chief Sirsky, could we touch base in the early afternoon for an update?" Becker asked.

"As you wish. To conclude this meeting, let's listen to Dominique Kreiss, who has more details about the murderer's profile."

"I am very curious to hear Miss Kreiss's opinion," Becker said, with what seemed like a note of sarcasm.

Not everyone accepted the practice of profiling. Nico thought this was unfortunate, but he was sure that more law-enforcement officials would come around. He was convinced that an understanding of a criminal's emotional makeup and motives were key to solving many crimes.

"I might be repeating myself, but let me restate the characteristics that the three victims shared," Dominique began, not at all perturbed by the disdain the magistrate had expressed. "First, our serial killer is meticulous and obsessive and chooses victims who are physically similar and have the same profile. When he amputates their breasts, he is acting out revenge against his mother. He is most likely a white male, as such killers often murder in the same ethnic group. He is twenty-five to forty years old, intelligent, and organized. He's familiar with police techniques and knows how to dissect and suture human tissue. There are also biblical connotations in the messages he leaves for us. 'Seven days, seven women' challenges the day of rest on Sunday. And then, 'Nico, I am shattering my enemies, and Sunday you will not be able to rise.' That brings us to Psalms 18, verse 38—'I shattered them, so that they shall not be able to rise: They fell under my feet.'"

"Other than having some biblical knowledge, what does that tell us?" Becker asked.

"Nothing very specific," Dominique Kreiss said. "Just that our man is hiding behind the Bible, using it to justify his criminal objectives. I have the feeling that our killer is a cultivated man, but he is not a real believer."

"What makes you say that?" Nico asked.

"A very religious person would have too much respect for the text to modify it and use it for his own purposes. This man doesn't care and dares God to stop him."

"There are also the thirty lashes with the whip," Nico said. "That must mean something specific. If we find out what that is, it could lead us to him."

"Maybe it marks an anniversary?" the psychologist suggested.

"Why not. So thirty years ago some major event occurred that changed the course of his life?"

"You mean he could have cut off the tail of a lizard or smothered his cat?" Kriven said. "That's like looking for a needle in a haystack."

"You're right," Nico said. "It is probably some micro-phenomenon that conditioned the killer, and we will never find any trace of it. However, we can't ignore the symbolism of those thirty lashes. We have to look and explore the past. Kriven, since you've got a critical eye for this kind of thing, you're responsible. Consult the papers back then. Maybe there's a news item."

Kriven sighed and nodded.

"I don't need to tell you that this is a race against the clock," Nico told his team. "Today, the killer is preparing to take a fourth victim."

"And we have until Sunday," Becker said. "After that, the killer could escape us entirely."

"We had better arrest him before Sunday," Cohen concluded.

Everyone turned to the deputy police commissioner.

"Sunday, he might have Nico in his sights. Let's not forget that," he added in a sober voice.

At six in the morning, Nico went into his office. There were some files waiting for him on his worktable. He spotted the medical records and the victims' photos print-ed out from Alexis's computer. It was all there. Kriven had not brought this evidence to their meeting, leaving Nico to manage the situation. He would forgive Kriven for this minor infraction; he knew he could count on him under any circumstances, and that was comforting in a risky job like theirs. He made a copy of the file, put the original in a sealed envelope, and ordered an officer to take it to Magistrate Becker right away. That relieved his conscience. No criminal was going to push him into any misconduct. Then he organized protection for Sylvie and their son, sending a team to their home. Afterward, he called his ex-wife to warn her. A sleepy, hoarse voice answered.

"Sylvie, I have something important to tell you, and I need your full attention," he said to wake her up.

He heard her grumble. She coughed to clear her voice. "What is it?"

"I'm working on an ugly case. The criminal might be coming after my family."

"Is that why Alexis called me earlier? He asked if I had made an appointment with him this afternoon."

"And did you?" Nico asked, even though he knew the answer.

"No way! I stopped seeing him as a doctor when my husband dumped me.

"Sylvie, I didn't dump you, and you know it."

They had this discussion on a regular basis. Sylvie always returned to the attack, twisting the truth and passing herself off as the victim. She often claimed that she had gotten rid of the two men who had wrecked her life, but he knew she felt a pain that would hound her until her dying breath. She felt betrayed by her own son, sure that he didn't love her as much as he loved his father. Nico had done everything he could to make things better. But Sylvie had been deeply and permanently wounded. For him, she was still the mother of his son. But today he had a problem that was more urgent than her long-standing resentments.

"In a short while, you and Dimitri will be placed under police protection. Two officers will be knocking at your door. Let them in. Do not leave home until you are told you can. Call Dimi's school, and tell them he will be absent until the end of the week."

"Until I'm told I can? I'm not going to stay locked up here for weeks."

As usual, Sylvie thought about herself first. Her egotism was limitless.

"Everything should go back to normal on Monday. Trust me."

"Do I have a choice?"

"Not really. Can you watch over Dimitri?"

"If he doesn't run off to you."

"Sylvie, this is not a joke."

"I hear your cops arriving."

She hung up. Nico did not react right away, and the ring tone resounded in his ear for a while. He thought about Caroline, about her gentleness and the obviously fine mind she had. She was nothing like Sylvie. He imagined her soft skin under his lips...

§ § §

Deputy Chief Rost and Commander Kriven arrived at Alexis Perrin's office. The doctor was around forty and of average height. He had pale skin and blond hair. He looked fatigued and anxious.

Marc Walberg, the forensic handwriting specialist, was with them. They asked Perrin to sit down, and Walberg dictated the murderer's two messages. With his left hand, Alexis wrote the words on a blank piece of paper. Walberg took the crime scene pictures from his briefcase and compared the A's and the B's. Then the expert picked up some prescriptions from the doctor's desk and noted that the writing corresponded with what the doctor had just written and didn't look anything like the killer's. The question, then, was whether Dr. Perrin could have disguised the shape of his letters when he committed the murders. However, Walberg's analysis revealed that the killer's handwriting was authentic. He concluded that Alexis Perrin could not be the author of the messages—which didn't mean that he wasn't the murderer. Rost called Nico immediately to tell him, while Kriven checked the doctor's online calendar. He had to find out if he had had earlier appointments with the three victims. Perrin said no, but he needed to make sure.

§ § §

Despite the early hour, specialists were hard at work at the Paris police forensics lab, 3 Quai de l'Horloge in the first arrondissement. Professor Charles Queneau greeted Commander Théron in person. He was the lab's director, and he wanted a full role in this investigation.

"We have conclusions regarding the rope," the scientist said. "Everything's identical—diameter, twists, strands, and color. The rope used to tie up the three victims came from the same batch. The contact lenses are the same brand and the same correction. The wearer was far-sighted. I collected DNA from each of the lenses, and we'll compare it with the victim's, using a genetic amplification technique that has excellent results with small samples. You'll have our conclusions in twenty-four hours. The same procedure is being done on the blond hair you sent us last night. Dr. Tom Robin is handling it."

This detail meant that Professor Queneau had put his best specialists on the case. He was taking the situation very seriously and wanted it to be known. Théron nodded in acknowledgement.

"The blood taken from Mrs. Chloé Bartes's mirror has DNA corresponding to the victim," the professor continued. "I'm sorry to say that it doesn't reveal anything else."

"Damn! Well, that was to be expected."

"However, we did pick up traces of talc on Mrs. Trajan's slippers."

"What do you mean?"

"You heard me. The talc comes from Triflex, which is a brand of surgical gloves. Your man was wearing a pair when he grabbed the slippers. There is always talc in the packaging. For that matter, manufacturers recommend that doctors remove the excess powder before they do surgery."

"It couldn't come from some another source?"

"This talc has specific characteristics. The medical laboratories that make surgical gloves publish the specifications. There is no doubt."

"Can you get these gloves easily?"

"It's professional material, but I suppose that someone with enough motivation could steal some. One last point: we have finished examining the brown hairs. What is interesting in studying hair is that even years later, you can detect traces of exposure to a whole bunch of foreign chemicals called xenobiotics."

"What?"

"These are molecules that are foreign to the organism, ranging from medication to pollutants. I can tell you that the person to whom that hair belonged is a regular user of amphetamines."

"Were you able to establish an age?"

"Impossible. Finding evidence of drug use in hair has even been done on mummies that are thousands of years old. Hair, unlike biological liquids and tissues, is not biodegradable. More important, we have the owner's genetic imprint. For the moment, it is not very useful. We would need to compare the DNA with another sample."

"OK, talc and amphetamines. That's already pretty good. I'll be waiting for news on the rest, professor."

"You can count on me. As soon as I have something, I'll call you."

Théron left the police lab perplexed. He decided to contact Nico before going to the hospital to question Valérie Trajan's husband. He wanted to let him know about the lab's findings right away. There was nothing that would push the investigation forward dramatically, but all the evidence, put side-by-side, would eventually lead to the murderer. He really wanted to give his boss the key to this mystery, because he knew it was a delicate situation. Nico had every right to be alarmed. In any case, Théron was glad he wasn't in Nico's shoes. He thought about his wife. She resembled the victims and Nico's ex-wife. Damn, he wanted to go home and take her in his arms. She would be preparing the kids' breakfast. This morning he would give anything to kiss her neck, underneath her thick mane of brown hair. To drive her crazy.

12

IMMEDIATE DANGER

There were days when the solitude weighed heavily on him, and today was one of those. He felt his anxiety growing. He was hot and then cold, and then he didn't really know. Above all, he was afraid. He was afraid of looking into the empty eyes of another dead woman—the eyes of a woman he didn't know or the eyes of a woman who meant something to him. Why was the murderer after him personally? He had gone over all the successful investigations he had handled. Most of those men were still in prison, although some had served their time and been released. Remembering their cases drove him into a dreary and violent world where it was often difficult to determine whether the criminal understood exactly what he was doing or whether some mental imbalance could be blamed. Still, he thought that leeway given to law-breakers because of their mental problems was sometimes excessive. With a sudden urge, he grabbed his cell phone. He called the number he had memorized.

"Saint Antoine Hospital, how can I help you?" an impassive female voice said.

"I would like to speak to Dr. Dalry, please."

"Hold on, please."

Silence. Then another voice.

"Yes, what is it?"

"I would like to speak to Dr. Dalry," he said again.

"She is busy. Is there something I can help you with?"

"It's personal. This is Nico Sirsky. Could you please put me through?"

"Let me see if that is possible. Please hold the line."

Silence again. Caroline was more difficult to contact than a cabinet member. This thought made him smile. He didn't care about rank-related propriety, but knowing that Caroline's calls were filtered was a sign of her importance and made her all the more attractive.

"Hello."

He started. There she was, with that soft, calm voice. He felt his heart accelerate. "Nico Sirsky here."

"Yes, hi. Was it a hard night?"

"We're doing what we can."

"You didn't go home, did you?"

"No. It was an all-nighter."

"You already looked tired. As your doctor, I'm not at all happy about that."

"It's a good sign that you are worried about my health."

"How is Alexis?" she asked, not reacting. "He wasn't in great shape either. I was going to call your sister."

"The situation is a little complicated. I'll explain it to you. Actually, I was calling to, uh—"

"Yes?"

"Well, perhaps, um—"

"You can tell me."

"Okay. Are you free for lunch today? I don't really have the time, but I would love to see you. Accept. Please. It's just that—"

"I finish my rounds around one this afternoon, and I'm off until Monday. I've put in too many hours."

"That's great. I'll wait for you at my office, okay?"

"Fine."

"Caroline?"

"Yes?"

"I'm happy that you can come. I need to talk to you."

She didn't answer. He hadn't hoped for an answer. He hung up.

§ § §

Alexandre Becker leafed through Professor Vilars's autopsy report while imagining her in white scrubs, the green waterproof smock, a surgical mask, cap, protective glasses, gloves, and boots. He knew the introductory formula by heart.

> I, undersigned Professor Armelle Vilars, chief medical examiner, sworn in by the Paris Court of Appeals, appointed by Mr. Alexandre Becker, investigating magistrate with the High Court of Paris, with the assignment to:
>
> - Describe in detail the corpse of Valérie Trajan, brought to the Institut Médico-Légal de Paris
>
> - Carry out a full autopsy in view of establishing the circumstances and cause of death and to look for any evidence of a crime or misdemeanor
>   Proceed with taking any samples required and to carry out any necessary tests
>
> - Make all observations that could be useful in uncovering the truth.

The victim's full identity followed, with a summary of the facts, the date and time of the autopsy, and the list of people present. The next section covered the examination of the body, including height, weight, eye and hair color, postmortem lividity related to the position in which the body was discovered, and any lesions from being tied up, whipped, and stabbed. The wounds were numbered one to thirty and described in detail.

The inspection of the body was enough to establish an approximate time of death, always a delicate exercise. Rigor mortis set in two hours after death, peaking at twelve hours and then dissipating over the next twenty-four hours. Lividity, or areas where the blood settled, began three to six hours after death. It disappeared under pressure in the first six hours and then entirely after forty-eight hours. After six hours, the corneas became covered with an opalescent veil, making it tricky to discern the patient's actual eye color. Body temperature was also an indicator of time of death. By studying these elements, Professor Vilars deduced that Valérie Trajan died at four on Wednesday afternoon.

Then she focused on the breasts, which had been replaced by those from the second victim, Chloé Bartes. The murderer had used surgical sutures and had handled the needle with the skill of a professional. Then the medical examiner took blood samples for a toxicology screen, along with urine, gastric content, and bile samples. She took two of each sample in case a second opinion would be required later on. The third step involved making large incisions with a scalpel on the thighs, arms, and back and under the shoulder blades to look for bruising.

The report continued with the rest of the autopsy details. Two techniques were generally used to access the abdominal and thoracic cavities. A Y incision was the most common. Armelle Vilars preferred a vertical median incision from just under the sternum to the pubis, removing the sterno-costal mass.

Magistrate Becker could then read the detailed description of what the doctor did. The heart and lungs were removed and sent to the anatomopathology lab. The specialist dissected and studied all the organs. The pregnancy was noted and described, and the embryo was removed. To finish up, Professor Vilars sawed open the skull after making sure there was no fracture. There was no subarachnoid hemorrhage or epidural hematoma. The brain was intact.

As with the two previous murders, the cause of death was stabbing. The knife was introduced violently, penetrating the abdomen, rupturing the vena cava and causing internal hemorrhaging. The victim then died in less than two minutes. Her organs were floating in blood, which explained why it felt like she had a distended belly when it was palpated. "Violent death, criminal in nature. Death from hemorrhaging, following a penetrating wound of vital organs by a knife. I certify, having personally carried out this assignment on this day at 2:15 a.m., that this report is sincere and truthful." So ended her analysis.

What was important? The three victims resembled each other. They were pregnant and had fairly pleasant lives. Other than the observation that the killer had some imperious need to humiliate his victims by whipping them and that he amputated their breasts, there had to be something else. But what? The kind of sutures used and the rigorous technique seemed to direct the investigation toward the medical world. A doctor? Why not Dr. Alexis Perrin, despite what Chief Sirsky thought? He would question him and soon have his own opinion. He picked up the three victims' medical files, which Sirsky had sent to him after they were extracted from Dr. Perrin's computer. The photos were eloquent; they followed the murderer step by step. Only the killer could have taken them.

§ § §

Daniel Trajan had experienced a serious emotional shock. His doctors agreed that he needed time to recover. He would probably remain in the hospital for several days. Commander Théron found him lying motionless in his hospital bed, an IV in his arm and an empty look in his eyes, undoubtedly because of the medication. Yet Théron had to question him. Of course, he had checked his alibi with the law firm he worked for. But perhaps, with a little luck, Trajan would know something. As he began the interview, Trajan stared at the white wall in front of him. He answered by shaking his head mechanically, and he had nothing to say. He didn't understand why his wife had been chosen. It must have been a mistake. Théron ended the questioning with a lump in his throat. It was hard not to feel compassion for this man, but there was no time for that. A detail, however, caught his attention. According to her husband, Valérie Trajan had never worn contact lenses.

§ § §

David Kriven stared intently at the computer in the office he shared with his team. The space was cramped and uncomfortable. They had given up complaining, focused as they were on their job of safeguarding others. Kriven was reviewing news stories from thirty years earlier—when he was only four. Thirty lashes, thirty years—perhaps it was some sort of anniversary. He was looking for something that could have occurred in Paris and possibly be a lead, maybe a similar crime. The Internet proved to be useful for this kind of investigation. Some newspaper archives were not accessible online, so he had sent three of his men to the library to go through the microfilm files. His eyes were dry from staring at the screen. If there were something to find, his team would uncover it.

§ § §

They were finding evidence, but it wasn't leading any-where useful. Nico was exhausted. But he had to con-tinue looking, at all costs. He put his head in his hands, closed his eyes, and massaged his temples, as if that were enough to give him energy. Then he heard steps in the narrow hallway leading to his office. The door opened. He looked up. It was Caroline. There she was, smiling at him. He stood and crossed his office to embrace her. Ignoring the risk, he pulled her to him and pressed his lips against hers. Nothing else had any importance. Kissing her was all that he wanted to do. She did not move away from him. He felt her touch his neck, and a shiver ran down his body. He pressed himself against her, feeling her shape through their clothes. He held onto her mouth for a long moment. He tasted her tongue, both furious-ly and gently. Even as they moved apart to catch their breath, they held onto each other. He kissed her neck. He had dreamed about this. He loved her smell and the heat of her skin. He was crazy about this woman.

§ § §

Magistrate Becker invited Alexis Perrin into his office. The doctor was quite a sight. His features were contorted, he was extremely pale, and his eyes were full of anxiety. Once seated, Perrin couldn't control the trembling in his legs. The man seemed to be falling apart.

"I have a few questions to ask you, Dr. Perrin, concerning these murders. Chief Sirsky has told me that you are related. You know that he is in charge of the case and that you have become involved. You have become implicated."

"Implicated?"

"That's right. The analysis of your computer files and your appointment list lead us to believe that you knew the three victims."

"That's wrong. I never saw them before. I was not their doctor. I don't know how their medical files ended up on my computer. I thought your specialists were looking into that."

"Relax. I'm just trying to understand."

"And what do you think I want? This whole thing is driving me crazy. Good God, I saw those pictures. And I haven't been able to think about anything else since. I didn't have anything to do with that."

"Nobody said you did. Could you just tell me how the last few days unfolded for you at work? I know about those fake appointments."

§ § §

He couldn't take his eyes off her. He was holding her hand. He was afraid she would disappear, like a dream. They crossed the Pont Saint Michel, walking toward the Rue Saint André des Arts. In the middle of the bridge, above the Seine, they stopped to kiss again. A tender embrace. They decided to grab a quick crêpe for lunch, as he had to get back to the office quickly. He suggested that they meet later. He couldn't do without her now.

§ § §

Alexandre Becker felt very uncomfortable with Dr. Perrin's story. If the man sitting in front of him was not the murderer, then the killer had an overflowing imagination. He glanced at the report that came from Marc Walberg, the forensic handwriting expert. The doctor was left-handed, like the criminal. But according to Walberg, their writing styles were very different. It didn't prove that the doctor was innocent, but it was a piece of information. True, there was evidence that cast suspicion on Perrin, but Becker couldn't believe that the doctor was guilty. If he was upset, it was undoubtedly because of the unbelievable nature of the events that were happening to him. So if he wasn't the man, who was?

§ § §

Their legs were intertwined under the table. The waiter brought them the crêpes they had ordered, along with a bottle of cider. Nico felt twenty years younger, as though he were still a student. He had often hung out in this neighborhood, splitting his time between Science Po and law school at the Sorbonne. She had gone to med school near Odéon, Jussieu, and Saint Antoine. Life was strange. Perhaps they had crossed paths on the sidewalk, in front of a gallery on the Rue Mazarine, because both of them had liked walking. He wished he had met her all those years ago, but then he wouldn't have had Dimitri. In any case, she was here now. He ate with one hand, and rubbed her knee with the other. His fingers moved a little bit up her thigh, along her silky stockings. He was breathing quickly. She smiled. He leaned forward and kissed her again.

They separated in front of 36 Quai des Orfèvres after exchanging their private cell phone numbers. Heavy-hearted, he watched her for a moment as she walked away. What he really wanted was to catch up with her, hold her against him, and never let go. But that was impossible. Duty called. And what a duty it was—a serial killer, a suspected brother-in-law, a personal threat, and a fourth victim to come. That was the story of his life. He tracked criminals and it was more than a job. It was a calling.

Kriven had traced Alexis's calendar back several years and had found no sign of the three victims. That confirmed what he had said: he did not know them and had never been their doctor. Nico called Magistrate Becker, who told him he had finished questioning Dr. Perrin. They once again reviewed the issues linked to the investigation and covered the clues. There was plenty to do and not enough to put a name on the person behind these terrible acts. Tension was rising. After hanging up, Nico joined Théron's group. The team members were busy on their phones. They were finding the ex-convicts he had put away, comparing their profiles with that of the killer, and checking their schedules. It was Herculean work. Furthermore, many had fallen off the map. For the division, this was another chase.

§ § §

She finished her shift. He was going to follow her. He wouldn't let her out of his sight along the gray hallways in the metro, in the crowded, noisy subway car, or out in the open air of the city's sidewalks. No matter how fast or slow she walked, he would stay at a distance, but not too far away. Why risk allowing her to escape? Of course, he knew where she was going; he could always find her again. But it was better this way. He liked this moment, savored the thought of the moment they would soon be sharing. She was very beautiful, like the others. He saw that in her way of walking, in the clothes she wore, and the signs of her success. In fact, he despised her. She had hurt him so much, and he had put up with it in silence. Today, it was over. He would take control. He was going to kill her. She stopped to pick up some groceries. Her arms were full when she entered her building and climbed the two flights. She nearly dropped everything as she slipped her key into the lock. Fortunately, he was there. He offered to help her and took one of the packages. She thanked him with a shy smile. She hesitated to let him in, but finally, politeness took over, and she invited him to follow her.

"It's okay if you don't want me to. I understand. I can just leave this on the landing."

"No, no, come on," she finally said.

Inside, he was gloating. He had convinced her of his good faith. He already felt like she had offered herself to him. His excitement was growing. He pushed the door behind him without closing it. He didn't want to frighten her now that he was nearly there. Once in the kitchen, he slowly took hold of the handkerchief in his jacket pocket. He positioned himself behind the woman, and with an abrupt, determined movement, he pressed the cloth against his prey's mouth and nose. Surprise kept her from reacting. When she began to fight back, it was too late, and the drug was already taking effect. Her muscles were going limp, her mind getting cloudy. She slipped onto the tile floor. He loosened his grip and made sure she was not acting. After locking the entrance door, he explored the apartment. He immediately found the table he would attach her to. It was perfect. He went to work.

He felt intense joy when she regained consciousness. Her eyes opened, looking around for some explanation. Then she realized that she was lying naked on the floor in the living room, her wrists attached to the coffee table. A wide piece of duct tape over her mouth kept her from screaming. She started moving frantically. He squatted and watched her. He looked so detached, her fears multiplied. Tears slid down her cheeks, which were red with effort. And then resignation took over. She was all his. He could do whatever he wanted with her. He would whip her. Thirty lashes that would leave their mark on her skin forever. Thirty lashes to celebrate the only anniversary he remembered. To get revenge, to make up for a lack of love, for wandering and for remorse. And who worried about his pain? Who had extended a hand to him? Who had held him? Nobody. The time for revenge was now.

§ § §

The day was coming to an end. Nico knew that everything possible was being done, that his teams were real professionals. Yet frustration and a sense of being ineffective were crowding his mind. Now he was imagining the killer's fourth victim. The usual time for the crime had come and gone; it was on everyone's mind, even though no one had said anything. Another woman might already be dead. He called Caroline. He couldn't leave headquarters, and he shyly suggested that she join him at his office. He was afraid she wouldn't like that; in any case, she seemed to understand the situation and accepted. She arrived a little later with a bag of sandwiches and soft drinks. But he was hungry for her. He pushed her up against the wall in his office and kissed her fiercely. He had to caress her skin. He slipped his hands under her shirt and ran them along her back. She was soft and warm. She pulled away. He was feeling a little embarrassed, and she was a little winded. They ended up devouring the food. And then he went back to work. She sat down in the armchair in front of him. He did not want her to leave. In theory, no one outside the division was authorized to remain on the premises without an official reason, but tonight he did not care about the rules.

Despite her presence, he dived back into his files, rereading the descriptions of the three murders and comparing the pictures. And he repeated the killer's messages over and over in his head, asking himself what he should be looking for underneath the surface. What was the relationship to him? Sometimes he dared to glance at Caroline. She would look back at him with such gentleness, he wanted to drown in it. She was there, simply there, and it felt really good. He would spend his third all nighter with her. It was nearly midnight when he heard running in the hallway. Kriven was white as a ghost and nearly screamed, looking like he needed to spit out what he had to say. The sight of Caroline startled him.

"Dr. Caroline Dalry, Commander David Kriven," Nico said. "You can talk, David."

"Gamby just called. It's completely crazy. A new medical file was just sent to Perrin's computer! It's clearly being hacked. Gamby is sending you everything by e-mail. It should be arriving now."

"What is it?"

"We are going to find out."

"Where is Alexis?"

"At home."

"He's not in front of his own computer, is he?"

"No, it's not him, Nico. I checked. An officer is with him at his apartment and hasn't left him alone for a second. Perrin couldn't sleep, and they didn't stop talking. The officer swears that your brother-in-law has not touched the computer. In any case, we are checking the files. If they come from him, we'll know it. There will be some trace."

A signal indicated a message was waiting. He moved the mouse and opened the file. Kriven was standing behind him.

"Are the men ready?" Nico asked.

"They are all here. Nobody went home tonight."

Nico felt a lump forming in his throat. No new murder had been reported. The victim probably hadn't been discovered yet. Horror of horrors, he was going to learn the victim's name from the killer.

"Rue Molière, in the second arrondissement," Nico said, his voice full of dread. "Isabelle Saulière."

"Isabelle Saulière?" Caroline let out, looking stunned. "That can't be."

FRIDAY

13

ISABELLE

The Louvre appeared with its statues, high reliefs, and stone garlands. They passed the Palais Royal, abandoned centuries ago by Richelieu's guards. The Comédie Française and the ghost of Molière saw them speeding by. The Avenue de L'Opéra, the Rue Sainte Anne, the Rue Thérèse, and finally they arrived at the Rue Molière. They stopped their cars in the middle of the street, blocking traffic. Nico looked up at the building's third floor. No lights were on; they were the first to get there. None of them showed their apprehension.

In the office, Nico had seen the blood drain from Caroline's face. She knew Isabelle Saulière. That he had understood immediately. More than ever, he wanted to get this bastard.

"Isabelle Saulière?" Caroline had let out, looked stunned. "That can't be."

He remembered her reaction, astonished and worried, but contained. She was not the type to lose control in front of other people. He loved her even more for that.

"You know her?" he had asked calmly.

"Yes. Yes, I think so. She's a nurse at the hospital. She works in my department. Unless it's someone with the same name."

Nico felt like the ground was opening under him, as though he were falling and falling. How could that be? Why? Was Caroline in danger? These questions were bouncing around in his mind. He had to go to the scene, but he could not leave Caroline alone.

"You will stay here," he said. "I'm going to call an officer to keep you company until I get back."

She looked at him, her eyes full of questions and stupefaction.

"Please. Do that for me. I don't understand exactly what is going on. I can't figure out the connection. I don't want anything to happen to you."

"Do you think that it could?"

"The killer I'm looking for is playing with my nerves and with those close to me. Why a nurse from your department? Strange serendipity. Just this morning, I didn't dare think I had a chance with you."

He managed to get a smile out of her.

"Of course I wanted to try my luck," he continued. "But I didn't know how you would react. Our man is a mind reader, or maybe it's just a coincidence. As long as I don't know, I'm putting you under police protection. David?"

"Yes?" the police officer answered, having heard every bit of the conversation. He looked at Caroline with respect.

"Wake up Cohen and Kreiss, and give them Isabelle Saulière's address. Call Magistrate Becker; something tells me he is still in his office. And warn Professor Vilars, so she can be at work within the hour."

His team was at the scene. Nico forced the door open and entered, followed by Kriven and Captain Vidal. Their first goal was to find the body. They walked slowly to the living room. She was there, attached to a huge coffee table. Once again, it was a macabre sight.

§ § §

She had been home for only an hour when the telephone rang. It was an urgent call from police headquarters. The killer had found a fourth victim, and Chief Sirsky wanted her at the scene. She pushed aside the sheets, which were damp from their sweat. Rémi grumbled.

"Jesus, you just got home. Did you tell your boss that you have a life too?"

"It's my job. I've got to go. There's a reason they're calling me."

"First we finish what we started. Then you'll go."

All he could think about was getting laid. She wasn't getting out of bed just to annoy him. She was starting to get fed up. Rémi, a veterinarian with dark good looks, was clearly needy and had chosen her to satisfy himself. She had barely walked in the door when he jumped on her. But she wanted something else. You couldn't build a solid relationship entirely on sex. He forced her to assume all kinds of positions she had never even imagined possible. Enough was enough, but she was afraid to tell him. She had seen glimpses of a shady, angry side of his personality. She closed the bathroom door behind her and heard him spit out some insults. That was another reason to clear out. She got ready as quickly as possible and arrived at the Rue Molière in no time. She didn't live very far and had driven fast. The teams at the scene sent her to the third floor. She read "M. et Mme Victor Saulière" on the door.

"Ms. Kreiss?" She heard a voice behind her.

She turned. Michel Cohen joined her at the door.

"This can't go on," he said. "We need to put an end to the slaughter. We already have four victims on our hands, and we are all going to get burned. Let's go in. Sirsky is waiting for us."

They found the police officers in the living room. The room was silent. They kept a respectable distance between themselves and the body to avoid interfering with the evidence collection.

"A message?" Cohen asked immediately.

"Behind you," Nico answered.

The deputy commissioner turned around. Bloody letters were spread across an ornate mirror: "For her and the others, and for you, Nico, I'm preparing wickedness, I conceive mischief, and I bring forth falsehood." Dominique Kreiss couldn't hold back an anxiety-filled murmur.

"I bet it's another psalm," she said, breaking the icy silence that had settled in again. "The way the sentence is phrased."

Magistrate Becker came in. He calmly inspected the room and frowned when he read the message.

"Clearly this man does not like you, Mr. Sirsky, no more than he likes women," he said dryly.

Now everyone was staring at the body. The killer had left a new clue that no one had dared to touch yet. It was best to let Magistrate Becker give the go-ahead.

"Okay, who's going to do it?" he asked.

"Go ahead, Nico," Cohen said.

With a gloved hand, Nico lifted up the envelope that had been placed on the victim's stomach. He opened it with care, trying to limit the damage. Inside was a yellowed press clipping. He removed it. It felt like time had stopped, and everyone held their breath.

"The court rules that the seven-year-old boy who killed his mother acted in legitimate self-defense," Nico read. The article was thirty years old to the week. "'I'm too little to die,' the child said to police."

"What the hell is that?" Cohen asked.

"Clearly an old news story," Nico answered.

"'A seven-year-old boy described to police the chain of events that led him to stab his mother to death. The woman was suffering from what psychiatrists called a major depressive disorder, and she had already tried to smother the child. The court ruled that his actions were self-defense.' The mother woke her son up, then picked up a pillow and held it against his face. 'I'm going to send you to join your uncle in heaven,' she said to the boy. He managed to escape. A chase around the apartment followed, and they ended up in the kitchen. He killed her. It was either her or him.'"

"There's your motive," Dominique Kreiss said. "He's handing it to us."

"Could it be that simple?" Kriven responded. "He just decides to lead us directly to him?"

"It can't be," Becker whispered, as if to himself.

"Why not?" the psychologist continued. "This kind of criminal has a deeply rooted desire to be caught. He wants to challenge the detectives, but at the same time, he wants them to stop him from forging ahead."

"There are no names in the article," Nico said. "Kriven, run with this. I want to know who that kid was and what he's become."

§ § §

Professor Armelle Vilars was ready for the latest victim. She had just left work, and now she had to go back. Better to just move into the morgue and demand the immediate construction of an on-site apartment, she thought as she returned to her job. It would be easier. There was so much to do. She was thinking about all the families waiting for the autopsy reports of loved ones so they could arrange the funerals and begin their mourning process. There were so many children, young adults, and old people she had to examine to unravel the mystery of their deaths. She carried with her visions of the bodies she had cut open with her scalpel and the organs she had dissected. She remembered every word shared with disoriented parents. Although she was a professional, ghostly visions slipped into her dreams from time to time, disturbing her sleep. She let out a loud sigh. It was hard to chase these glum, nearly morbid thoughts from her mind.

"A heart that sighs has not what it desires," said someone behind her.

She started and spun around. Eric Fiori.

"What are you doing here?" she asked, a little angrily.

"My job. I'm staying late to catch up."

"That's up to me to decide."

"Don't worry, I won't ask for overtime. Consider it volunteer work."

"That's not how things are done here, Eric. I don't know what's gotten into you lately, but I'd like you to start following the rules. I won't tolerate any more misconduct from you."

The blow struck home, and the man's face went pale. He tightened his lips and shot her an angry look.

"I'm sorry," he managed to get out. "Since I'm here, is there anything I can do to help?"

"I already have things organized. I don't need you."

"Listen, Armelle, it's true I've been a little on edge. You can blame some personal problems I've had. I promise to fall back in line. Let me work with you tonight."

She looked at him. His mood had changed. He looked pitiful, as though he sincerely wanted to make up for his attitude. She wasn't going to lay it on and push things all the way to humiliation. She preferred peace to underlying tension.

"Okay, stay. The fourth victim should arrive any minute now and is going to take some time."

"Thank you."

§ § §

Nico's cell phone rang out in the car that was taking them to the medical examiner's office.

"Chief Sirsky?"

"That's right."

"Professor Charles Queneau."

It was the director of the police forensics lab in person.

"I have interesting results. I know that time is of the essence, so I wanted to give them to you right away."

"I'm listening, Professor."

"The DNA lifted from the two contact lenses didn't come from just the victim, Valérie Trajan. On the lens taken from Madame Trajan's left eye, there was DNA from two different people: her and somebody else. On the second lens we found only the DNA of that other person. I then compared it to the brown hair. The conclusion is astonishing. The person the hair came from and the other person whose DNA was on the lens are clearly related."

"Related?"

"Exactly. We are looking at two people—it's impossible to tell if they are male or female—from the same family. Meanwhile, the blond hair we tested at your request belongs to Dr. Perrin. And finally, the blood used to write the message came from the victim. I hope this helps."

"I'm sure it will, Professor. Thank you. I'll keep you posted."

They ended the call. Cohen and Becker gave him questioning looks. He relayed the conversation.

"Imagine the mother and the son," Nico said, referring to the news clipping they had found earlier.

"She's dead," Becker said.

"He could have kept a lock of her hair," Nico said.

"From when he was seven?" Cohen asked.

"And why not?" the chief insisted. "We've seen worse. The boy, now an adult, is seeking revenge against the mother who betrayed him. He is killing her over and over again. I'm sure that all the victims look like her, a rather beautiful brunette. At least that is the image he holds onto."

"So, what do you have to do with this story?" Cohen asked.

"I don't know," Nico said, discouraged.

"Maybe he's targeting your position," Cohen continued.

"Could be," Nico said. "But it feels very personal."

"Last stop, all passengers please exit," Cohen interrupted.

The morgue rose in front of them, its red brick walls standing out against the sky. Most Parisians knew where they would end up but couldn't imagine what went on in this building. And that was just as well.

§ § §

In her tiny office, Dominique Kreiss was logged onto the Internet, looking for a full list of the psalms.

"That's it," she said to herself.

Psalm 7, verse 14 appeared on her screen. "Behold, he travails with wickedness, and he conceives mischief and brings forth falsehood." Incredible. The killer had put himself into the text. Dominique thought about the news clipping and the story of the little boy. Using the term "brings forth" was not an accident. Perhaps the killer was referring to his mother, who brought forth evil by giving birth to him. And he, in turn, begot evil, an unbroken chain. He was clearly experiencing a deep-seated feeling of guilt, that of having been forced to kill his own mother in order to survive. Who could withstand that kind of trauma? Life sometimes holds strange trials.

§ § §

Kriven and his men were moving heaven and earth. They had contacted the police station in charge of the investigation thirty years earlier, when the boy murdered his mother, and now they were at work searching through their archives. As soon as they found the file, they faxed it to headquarters.

"The boy's name was Arnaud Briard, seven years of age," Kriven read. "His mother, Marie Briard, died at the age of twenty-six. She worked in a bar before turning to prostitution to raise her son. Her parents had cut off all communication with her when they discovered that she had gotten pregnant by a stranger. There you have it, an ordinary story. It's up to us now to find out what became of the young Arnaud. He would have been placed in a foster home in the Paris area. We don't have any information after that. The local police will send us pictures.

The men were dismayed and disconcerted. The criminal—if it was, in fact, the boy all grown up—could suddenly have a face and a background that was too much to bear. Their eyes held a mixture of pity and rage.

"Let's go," Kriven said. "Squads five and six, I want to know everything there is to know about Marie Briard, from where she was born to where she is buried. Let's see if we can find some witnesses. The other squads will take Arnaud. What has he become? Where is he today? If he's still alive, bring him to me. If he's the killer, I want to know. Now get to work."

§ § §

Marc Walberg stared at the message written in blood. He was entirely focused. The killer was completely crazy, and he was getting worse; he was losing his grip on reality and the social conventions he had observed with so much skill until now. Walberg drew these conclusions from the changes in his handwriting. The killer was now trying, consciously or not, to disguise his writing. The letters were more curved, and the dots on the i's were rounder instead of small and restrained, giving them a feminine appearance. And yet, it was the same person. He was sure of that. For that matter, he had a theory about what was happening. The killer was imitating someone very dear to him, in this case, a woman. He took a number of pictures, from a distance and close up to capture every letter. Now he had to write up his report and give it to Sirsky.

§ § §

Nico could not stop staring at the rigid body covered with wounds and bathed in its own blood. Nico remembered a woman he had met a few years earlier who was initially intrigued by his work. She wanted to know everything about his day-to-day experiences. Nico had recounted it all—the victims, the aggressors, the blood, the horror. In the end, she had left him, repulsed by the smell of death she perceived when she was close to him. Things were different with Caroline. He felt he could talk to her without fearing that she would be driven away, and he did need to talk to her. That was what it would take to build a solid relationship. She was a doctor, so he hoped she would understand better, would know how to keep things in their place. His cell phone rang in the middle of the autopsy. Cohen and Becker started, while Professor Vilars remained impassive. He moved away to answer.

"Professor Charles Queneau here. Is this a bad time?"

"No, go ahead. Do you have something new?"

"Yes. We have just finished comparing the DNA found on the contact lenses with the brown hair. I told you they were related."

"So?"

"We proved the relationship, thanks to mitochondrial DNA, which is only transmitted from mother to child."

"Good work!"

"I'll get all that down on paper for you and send you the report within the hour."

"Thank you, Professor. This confirms our assumptions and is very useful."

"I'm glad to hear it."

Nico hung up and returned to Isabelle Saulière's autopsy. He told his colleagues about the forensic team's conclusions.

"The noose is tightening, Nico," Cohen said. "We're going to get him. I hope before this afternoon."

"Before this afternoon." Nico knew what his boss was saying: "before there is a fifth victim."

14

MOTHER AND SON

Summer seemed to be lingering. The weather stayed sunny and hot, sustaining the festive atmosphere in Paris. The back-to-school season had already brought its lot of traffic jams and busy people, but the light gave the city the feeling of a seaside resort. He was quite simply happy with his hand in hers, as if they were alone in the world. He imagined her smiling at him. She could give him one of those kisses on the cheek that only she knew how to give. But she wouldn't. She couldn't anymore; she lived in a world where there was no room for anyone else, a world without a future. He knew that, but what could he do? He wasn't strong enough to get her out of there, and this very thought filled him with a deep sense of sadness.

He held her thin hand a little tighter without getting any reaction. She didn't feel anything anymore, not even love for him. How long had it been like this? Several months. For months she had gone out at night, coming back in the early morning looking spent, her makeup smeared on her pale cheeks. Without saying a word, she would take a shower and go to bed to hide under the covers. She didn't even look at him.

He was so afraid. A long moment went by. He continued to sit on the floor, near the bed, until she woke up again. There had been so many nights filled with anxiety. One day, he would have a good job and would get her out of here. He was a smart boy with a promising future.

Then she would be treated like a queen and would get her revenge for these hard times. But she had shooed away this promise of his. She didn't believe him. She had killed their dream.

He was still holding her hand. She was walking quickly. She had picked him up after school, something she hadn't done for a long time. Was everything going to go back to the way it was before? Would she love him again? That was what he wanted more than anything else. He tried to get her attention, to stop her and hug her. She was so beautiful to him. But it was futile. There was a determination in her walk that he hadn't seen in a long time. They went home to their apartment in the dirty gray building. It had once been decorated with taste. Strangely, she had set the table. The place smelled good. Something was masking the old cigarette odor he had gotten used to. His favorite chocolate cake was next to his plate. But the place was still a mess, with empty liquor bottles scattered around the floor, the ashtray overflowing. She sat him down and served him. The evening was starting off well, and he began to think that maybe everything was going to go back to normal. It was just that her hands wouldn't stop shaking, her crazy look kept inspecting everything, and her thin, stiff body had something pathetic about it.

He ate dinner, but she didn't touch her food. She sent him to bed. As he lay under the covers, a dull worry kept him from going to sleep. When he finally did doze off, the dreams followed each other. In one he felt her caresses calming his body and soul, while in the next he couldn't even recognize the woman leaning over him, desperate, nearly mad.

A nightmare or reality, everything changed so suddenly. He had killed her with his own hands. Then he had left the apartment and walked down the filthy hallway to the neighbors, a retired couple. He knocked on the door. She was the one who opened up, lowering her wrinkled face to look at him, surprised to see him at such a late hour. She had often mussed his hair and given him candy. He liked the hard candies in all different kinds of colors. This thought warmed him a little, but only for a moment. The burning terror quickly gripped his body and his mind, and he was overwhelmed with the guilt, and the sense that he was lost forever.

"I killed her," he managed to mumble.

The old woman knit her eyebrows and leaned forward. She hadn't heard his confession. He cleared his throat.

"I killed Mommy," he said in a plaintive voice.

She stared at him, unable to accept what he had said. Time stopped. The first tears formed in the child's eyes. It was at that moment that she believed him.

"Dear God in heaven. Roger, Roger!" she cried out.

Her husband ran to her, frightened, and she sent him to the little boy's apartment.

When he returned, his face was pale, and he called the police. Two officers arrived very quickly. They took notes. Their investigation did not last long. The culprit was there and confessing.

The police officers were dumbfounded and contacted their superior, who then arrived.

"Will I go to prison?" the boy had asked, so serious.

"Don't know—don't think so," the chief had managed to say. He had never faced this kind of situation before.

He asked the old couple if the kid had any other family. No, they didn't think he did. The poor little guy was now all alone.

The next day, the story was in the local section of the paper. The following day, a few reporters developed it for the front page. The evening news ran with it. The boy remembered that she had screamed at him, had declared that the world was a rotten place and that she wanted to send him to heaven; he would be better off there. He didn't agree. He had managed to reach the kitchen and grab a long knife. He killed her as she threw herself at him. He said he was "too little to die." These words made the headlines. He was placed in foster care. Then the reporters stopped talking and writing about him. The story died, and he remained alone with his suffering.

He missed his mother so much.

§ § §

A drug addict was what she had become, what she was trying to hide from others and herself. To fill the growing emptiness and calm her anxiety, she had upped her intake of antidepressants. Her therapist kept telling her that her feelings were temporary, that she had what it took to get through this hard time. All she needed was patience. Right now she wanted to let everything go, to run away from her responsibilities and disappear forever. She was thinking about suicide, especially when she couldn't sleep in the early morning. Why resist? For her son, of course. Wasn't that enough? But Dimitri only had eyes for his father. She was sure she loved Dimitri, but she was incapable of showing him. She remembered when he was little, crawling on all fours, his blond hair a mess as he babbled happily. He was so handsome! What remained of those times? If it were up to him, he would be living with his father full time. Nico, the love of her life, had left her. He had never really loved her. He could have taken his son from her a thousand times, but he hadn't done that. As usual, he was decent. Did he even suspect what condition she was really in? The answer was no, or he would have been there to protect Dimitri and take charge. Damn it! She was going to tell him. Why spare him? She needed a helping hand, *his* helping hand.

§ § §

At five in the morning, he walked into his office with rare eagerness. It had nothing to do with the urgency of his job. He was thinking about Caroline. She was there, dozing in one of the leather armchairs. The patrol officer was sitting in another chair, reading a magazine. Nico signaled to him to leave them alone, but he asked him not to go far. Their whispering had not awakened her. He nuzzled her neck, smelled her, and caressed her lips. He felt her arms wrap around him and her fingers settle on his neck. Her mouth sought his. His heartbeat accelerated. He wanted her. He pulled back, uncomfortable, and looked into her bright eyes. She knew. She stretched, trying to wake up completely, and her movements were sensual. She couldn't have been more attractive.

The phone rang, breaking the silence. It was his mother, Anya. She never called this early.

"Nico, I'm really sorry to bother you."

"What's happening? Something serious?"

"No, don't worry. Well, it could become serious. Your son just called me."

"Dimitri?"

"You only have one, as far as I know. He's worried about Sylvie. She hasn't been acting normal, and he thinks she is at the end of her wits. He needed to talk about it."

"Why didn't he say anything to me?"

"You are always trying to defend her. He was worried that you wouldn't believe him and that you would blame the usual little disagreements. He says she is taking medication, a lot of medication. She cries a lot and barely talks to him anymore."

"Damn!"

"In any case, he wants to be with you. You asked him to stay out of school this week, so you should try to pick him up this morning."

"I don't really have the time. But I can't leave things like this."

"Nico, I'm not sure that Sylvie is in any condition to take care of him. You should reconsider the living situation. It's no longer healthy for him, and it is disturbing him more than you think. What I want more than anything is to protect my grandson. You couldn't bear it if anything happened to him, could you?"

"Okay, I'll take care of it."

"I can if you want. I'm at your sister's place. We could swing by and pick up Dimitri."

"No, don't go anywhere. I'll take care of it. It's my responsibility."

"Perfect. Keep me posted. You know I'll fret."

§ § §

They would know the truth. It was just a matter of time. He had managed to hide his past for all these years, and now he was going to have his entire life spread out for everyone to see. How was that possible? How did this happen? He should have known that the time would come. He had committed a sin of pride, thinking he could fool the world until his last breath. What did he feel? It was hard to define. He felt a huge emptiness, like an icy coldness piercing his body and his soul. He felt the fear of finding himself alone again, as he had on the day that was forever engraved in his mind. But he also felt some relief at not having to act out the sure-of-himself role any longer. He could shed the past he had created out of thin air to keep people off his scent. Slumped in his office chair, he waited for it to catch up with him. All he could do was stay there and do nothing. The phone rang. He answered.

"Sir, Chief Sirsky is here. He would like to see you. Should I let him in?" his secretary asked.

§ § §

Thirty years had gone by, too much time to find all the witnesses in the Briard case. The professor of child psychiatry who had cared for the young Arnaud had died. Fortunately, the hospital in Evry had preserved all its archives. Kriven had sent a patrol unit. He was now reading the medical file. The doctor had underlined the "extreme rarity" of this kind of murder. "I do not think that it is possible to find a single incident of matricide by a child in the psychiatric journals," the psychiatrist wrote in his introduction. "In forty years of practice, I have encountered five or six cases of child criminals, but none like this. Underage criminals are most often teenagers." Then came the doctor's conclusions:

> I am struck by Arnaud's maturity. The mother
> was depressive and probably decided to put an end
> to her days after doing away with her child. The
> care that Arnaud gets must allow him to process
> his feelings of guilt. He needs help to move on. He
> needs someone to listen to him. His psychothera-
> peutic support should be as sensitive to his needs
> as possible and should never resemble any kind of
> interrogation. This child has already suffered from
> being asked too many questions. The effects on his
> mental health are unclear. He could experience
> depression or attempt suicide; no possibilities should

be excluded. On the other hand, he could get past this. Forgetting would be desirable. That, however, doesn't seem likely.

"David?"

It was the second-ranking detective in the squad, Amélie, a young woman with a promising future.

"Yes? Do you have something?"

"I found the court report. As the article mentioned, the court in Evry ruled self-defense. A juvenile judge was appointed to oversee the support measures ordered to protect Arnaud Briard. His maternal grandparents didn't want him. They had not seen their daughter since she left the family home, and they did not know their grandson. The boy was placed with child services. It was impossible to find a family to take him, despite the recommendation from the court-appointed doctor and the judge."

"Did you contact the group facility?"

"Not yet."

"Be quick about it. I want to know where Briard is today."

§ § §

Bastien Gamby was annoyed. He was the best computer specialist there was and had skills that foiled top terrorist plans. The Quai des Orfèvres counter-terrorist section did everything it could to keep him on board. And here was some serial killer making his life difficult. He had tried everything, but he couldn't find the source. He knew how the murderer introduced the data, but he couldn't identify where it came from. He was ready to blow his top, despite his natural calm in just about any circumstance. He wanted to break something.

The screen was blinking. A woman's smile appeared. What was this bullshit? He typed on the keyboard. A new medical file arrived. He opened it.

"This can't be!" he bellowed.

§ § §

He didn't call her because he wanted to, but rather because he was afraid that her depression was endangering their son. If Sylvie really was going through a tough time, the worst could happen.

"Sylvie, it's Nico."

"Nico? What's gotten into you to call at this hour? I'm sure it's not because you care about me. Let me guess. You want to talk about your son. You're worried, which is normal, considering what a bad mother I am."

"Sylvie, stop. I'm starting to get fed up with resolving your day-to-day issues. I have other things to do, believe me."

"Oh. Yes, please excuse me, sir chief of police. I forgot how important you are to the country's security!"

"Don't take that tone with me. I'm calling because I know that you haven't been feeling yourself lately, and what you just said confirms it. I should have noticed earlier. What's wrong, Sylvie? What's going on?"

"What's wrong? Well shit! Life is great, can't you tell?"

Nico closed his eyes and rubbed his face with a weary hand. The suspicions shared by his mother and Dimitri were founded. He felt deep sadness for his ex-wife. How could he help her get through this? No, he didn't have any feelings for her anymore, but she was the mother of his son, and he was determined to take that into account, despite his exasperation. Yet what he really wanted was to focus on rebuilding his life and shedding the burden that she represented.

"Sylvie," he said quietly, "Are things that bad for you?"

"Yes." She let out a nearly inhuman cry. "I need to get away for a while, Nico. I'm drowning. I can't find anything to grab onto."

"Your son…"

"You are everything to him. Can't you finally admit that? I don't know what to do anymore. I don't know what to do or say."

"So what's the solution?"

"Take him full time."

"But what are you going to do?"

"I have to get help. I'm on antidepressants during the day and sleeping pills at night; I'm going around in circles. I don't have the energy to take care of him anymore. I can't even stand to see him in the morning when I manage to wake up, because I see you, Nico. I have to do something. Give me some time. And don't go and say that you've got a problem taking your son."

"Sylvie, I've met someone."

There was no response, just Sylvie's throaty breathing and then a muffled sob. He felt a light hand on his shoulder. Nico finally opened his eyes. Caroline was standing near him. He leaned his forehead against her stomach, and she ran her hand through his hair.

"Sylvie…"

"Is it serious?"

"Yes."

"The *great* Nico finally fell for someone. You're in love. She must really be out of this world."

"She is."

"Good. I'll drive Dimitri to your place today. You can tell your henchman to stay with him until you get back, can't you? I'm talking about that cop who's been on our asses for I don't know what reason."

"Okay, but you have to stay under police protection until the end of the investigation."

"Whatever. But I don't want anyone underfoot, not right now. I think we've said everything there is to say. I'll let you know when I'm feeling better."

"What can I do to help?"

"Nothing. Nothing at all. You are the last person I should count on. See you someday, Nico."

"Good luck, Sylvie."

She hung up first. He had just turned a page in his life. He drew Caroline to him, tenderly.

"Kiss me," he said.

She did. He held her in his arms and forgot the world around them.

§ § §

He hadn't managed to sleep. That was not a good sign. He couldn't control the flow of his thoughts anymore. He needed to kill, again and again. How could he explain that? He had read so much about it, sought the opinions of the best psychiatrists. It was the result of accumulated childhood traumas. It stemmed from his parents' poor influence: an absent father and a domineering, castrating mother who treated her son like a partner. Blah, blah, blah. What bullshit. He accepted himself as he was and dealt with his urges. He enjoyed killing. The reasons mattered little. And he would continue to kill. Challenging Nico Sirsky and targeting what was dearest to him added spice to everything. The bastard would end up being a shadow of himself. Because he knew his weak point.

§ § §

The phone interrupted their kiss. Nico wasn't thinking very clearly anymore. Caroline pulled away from him and sat down in the armchair on the other side of the desk.

"Nico? It's Kriven. Something crazy just happened. A new medical file just came up on Perrin's computer."

"Jesus. The fifth victim?"

"Not at all."

"What do you mean, David?"

"*Your* record, Nico! The one from Saint Antoine Hospital."

15

THE FIFTH VICTIM

A chill ran through him. His adrenaline shot up, accelerating his heartbeat.

"What?" he managed to ask.

"Your visit to the hospital, the name of the doctor, your
endoscopy, the results. It's all there," Kriven answered.

"That's impossible!"

"For Gamby, it's child's play to get into the hospital's
network. Except that our man would have needed to
know that you had an appointment."

"What does it mean, other than he's thumbing his nose
at me and demonstrating that he knows exactly what I'm
doing?"

"I don't know. But it has to mean something."

"Was Gamby able to track it to the source?"

"No, believe it or not. He's going crazy. He can't trace
it. There's no way."

"So this guy is really skilled."

"That's for sure. He knows quite a bit about computers.
He installed all the necessary obstacles and covered any
tracks that could lead to him. Gamby is working away
at it furiously. He's taking this personally. It's a blow to
his ego."

"And as far as Isabelle Saulière is concerned?"

"Nothing promising yet."

"Briard?"

"We're going to find him soon, believe me."

"Thirty minutes, that's what you've got. Then I want everyone in my office. Spread the word."

§ § §

Sitting in her office, Captain Amélie Ader stared in disbelief. She had found it—his record, with his picture and his name. It had to be a mistake. It couldn't be possible. Unless… Unless the man she was looking at was, in fact, the criminal they had been tracking for more than four days. Weren't sociopaths very skilled at deceiving the people around them? If this was their man, who could you trust? It would be a real blow if the killer were an eminent member of their own ranks.

She mentally reviewed her investigation of the young Arnaud Briard. She had been trying to find out what had happened to him. He had gone from one facility to another, one school to another until he was eighteen. And then he had disappeared. What had become of him? Then it had occurred to her that he might have taken on another identity. It would have been easy enough. As soon as he turned eighteen, all he had to do was apply for a name change because of the hardship his real name presented. An application would have been sent to the Garde des Sceaux, and a legal announcement would have appeared in the *Journal Officiel*. In the end, the Procureur de la République would have rectified the official records. Good-bye Arnaud Briard. A new identity, a new life.

Having finally obtained that grown-up name, Amélie Ader read and reread it. She still couldn't digest this information. It was time to get her superiors in the loop. She couldn't wait to see their faces.

§ § §

Kriven was looking at the pictures of Marie Briard and her son. The serial killer's victims didn't really resemble the mother. And Arnaud looked like a good-natured kid, with blond hair and blue eyes just like his mother's. It was hard to imagine that this boy was committing such crimes thirty years later. When he examined the boy's features, he had a strange impression that they looked familiar. So where was this Arnaud Briard hiding today? What was he doing while Kriven's team was trying to get its hands on him? And why Nico's medical file? What did he want with that? He was more worried about it than his boss was.

Kriven was lost in his thoughts and started when he heard, "Commander?"

He looked at the woman who was working at a neighboring desk.

"Yes, what have you got?"

Amélie nodded with a serious look. David Kriven understood immediately that she had found something.

"You'll never guess in a million years. It's no wonder we never found Arnaud Briard. He changed his name."

"Changed his name?"

"Exactly."

"So? Come on, Amélie, spit it out!"

"Believe me, you'd better sit down."

§ § §

The sun had risen, casting a pale glow over the city. He had allowed Caroline to go home, but in an unmarked police car with two officers. She wanted to take a shower and change her clothes. He wished he could have gone with her. He was feeling lonely now. It was a strange sensation. A group of officers burst into his office without knocking, surprising him. Deputy Chief Rost led the way, followed by Commander Kriven and his second in command, Amélie Ader, a small, pretty brown-haired woman. Commander Théron and Dominique Kreiss brought up the rear. They all had dark circles under their eyes and looked drawn and pale.

"You wanted something new. Well you are going to get it!" Rost said.

"Did you find Arnaud Briard?" Nico asked.

"We sure did!" Kriven said. "Amélie found the needle in the haystack. She's got quite a sixth sense."

"Right, that sixth sense," Nico said. "That's what you're paid for, isn't it? So? Where is he?"

"Not far," Rost said.

The deputy chief handed his superior a white piece of paper folded in half.

"It's like the Oscars," he said. "It's written inside. A small detail: Briard changed his name, which is why we had a hard time finding him. Hold on tight."

Nico unfolded the paper and stared at the letters written in blue ink. He swallowed hard.

"Incredible. Are you sure?"

"There's no mistake," Captain Ader said.

"The A for Arnaud and the B for Briard. It makes sense," Nico said.

"What are you going to do?" Kriven asked.

"I'm going to go see him immediately. Find out everything you can about him—his schedule since Monday, his medical history, DNA, family. I want everything right now. Amélie?"

"Yes?"

"Good job. Why don't you go home and rest. You deserve it."

"There's still a lot to do, Chief. I would prefer to stay."

"It's an order, Captain. We're going to need fresh troops, so obey. Come back when you've had some sleep. You're not looking so good."

"I don't want any special treatment. If it's because I'm a woman…"

"Damn it!" Nico interrupted. "Don't argue. Get out of here."

The young woman disappeared, resigned but looking forward to a few hours of rest.

"What else?" Nico asked.

"Gamby is working like a mad man," Kriven said.

"We have DNA of the presumed killer and his mother. That's key," Rost continued. "We'll be able to compare it with our suspect. The thirty lashes could correspond to the anniversary of Marie Briard's death."

"It looks like the murderer's profile is clear now," Dominique Kreiss said. "We need to pay attention to the change in his behavior. The man is no longer in control, and he is losing contact with reality, as we saw in Marc Walberg's handwriting analysis. The last message showed characteristics of a woman's writing. His declining mental state makes him even more dangerous, but at the same time, he could make a mistake. He is more vulnerable. I have to call the psychologist at the last institution Arnaud Briard was sent to. He is still working."

"There is nothing as far as Isabelle Saulière is concerned," Théron said. "I don't see anything in her private or professional life worthy of further attention."

"I'm not surprised," Nico said. "The only commonality among the four victims, other than their appearance and their social status, was that they were pregnant. How, for God's sake, did the killer have access to that information? I want to know."

"Perhaps he will tell you," Kriven said.

"Perhaps, indeed. Let's get back to work. We still have a lot on our plates."

"Do you want someone to go with you?" Rost asked.

"I don't think so. If he put so much energy into hiding his past, he won't confide to a whole assembly. It's better that I deal with him man to man, before word gets out. I'll let Cohen know what I'm doing, and I'll fill you in as soon as possible.

Nico left 36 Quai des Orfèvres. It had turned cold. His jacket was back in his office, and his suit didn't do much to protect him from the rain that was beginning to fall. But actually, he didn't mind this kind of weather. He had grown up in northern France, and his childhood stories were filled with rain, snow, and icy winds. He headed toward the Palais de Justice entrance on the Rue de Harlay, just a few steps from headquarters. The short walk perked him up. Before he knew it, he was in the hallways, walking past doors protected by overworked secretaries. His badge gave him authority, hastening him through the security checks.

§ § §

He answered the phone mechanically.

"Sir, Chief Sirsky is here. He'd like to see you. Should I let him in?" his secretary announced.

"Yes, and bring some coffee, please," he said in a shaky voice.

It was all happening just as it had in his dream.

Nico came in. The man had changed. He was slumped in his chair, his face hollowed and his eyes looking into the distance. He had lost his arrogance and the authority that went with his rank. There was infinite sadness in his face, probably due to remorse. Nico swallowed hard, feeling afraid. And what if it were true? Magistrate Alexandre Becker's hair was brown, unlike the boy's hair in the picture Nico had in his pocket. And his eyes were brown, not blue. But there was a resemblance. The features were similar, aged by thirty years.

"I was expecting you sooner or later," the magistrate said in a voice full of emotion.

"How should I take that?" Nico asked.

The magistrate gave him a tight smile. "It was just a matter of time," he said in a final attempt to affirm his authority.

His shoulders slumped a little more. Nico saw tears form in the corners of his eyes, but the man held them back.

"I don't really understand. Help me out here," the chief said.

"That article. When you read it out loud, I thought I was going to have a panic attack. I couldn't say anything. I couldn't believe it. It took so much effort to detach myself from the past, to erase it from my mind, as if it were not really my story. What a mistake. How can you forget where you come from? Everything came flying back at me. I had suffered, but I had managed to come through. Now my life is destroyed."

"So you are Arnaud Briard?"

"Why deny it?"

"Your mother tried to kill you," Nico said, thrown off by his willing admission.

"Yes. I still see her chasing me, her face crazy. The drinking, the drugs. I learned about the prostitution later. She had hit rock bottom, and there was nothing I could do."

"You were just a child."

"And do you think that excuse is enough for me? I loved my mother. And we loved each other, until she broke down. I had become a burden for her, all the more so because her family had rejected her."

"I'm so sorry. That must have been very hard."

"It was. I grew up alone. But I wouldn't have become what I am today. It gave me the determination I needed to hang on and build a life for myself."

"And today?"

"Today, I have two children. Did you know that?"

"Not until now."

"I'm married. I have built a family that I love. I give my loved ones the affection that I didn't get. It is what I've done best, Chief Sirsky. I doubted for so long that I could lead a balanced life and have normal relationships. I fought for that. Oh, sometimes the nightmares take me back thirty years. I see the knife plunging into my mother's body, that look of disbelief on her face before she collapsed on the floor, and I cry. But I have managed to overcome it."

"Really?"

"If you are asking if I killed those women, then the answer is no. How could I have done that?"

"You already did it once."

"That was low. I am not a murderer. You cannot make assumptions about me, based on my past."

"There was that newspaper clipping about you and your mother on the body of the last victim."

"It's a trap. The killer wants to throw us off. He's mocking us. Didn't I trust you about your brother-in-law?"

"We will have to compare your DNA. An investigation is under way. I'm going to have to ask you some questions."

"Can we keep things quiet?"

"You have enough experience to know that some kinds of information are hard to hide."

Alexandre Becker nodded.

"This may not be easy for you, but where is your mother's body?"

"It was cremated. Her family did not want to bury her. There isn't even a place where I can go visit her."

"Did you keep anything belonging to her?"

"I know where you are going with this: the brown hair. My mother was blond. It is simply impossible. And no, I don't have anything of hers, except a few pictures. Keepsakes that might be important when you're thirty aren't necessarily important when you're seven. And nobody suggested that I take any with me, either."

"We'll need your schedule for the week."

"Particularly at the time of the murders, I suppose. I might as well tell you everything. I received an anonymous phone call on Monday telling me that my family had just had a serious car accident. I ran to the hospital, but no one was there. My wife was at work, and my kids were at school. I know it sounds crazy, but it's true."

"And Tuesday?"

"The school called me. My son had just fallen, and the principal thought he might have a concussion. He asked me to come and get him."

"Was it another false alarm?"

"Exactly. It's similar to your brother-in-law, with his fake appointments."

"The same thing happened on Wednesday and Thursday, I suppose?" Nico asked.

"Yes," Becker muttered, looking worried.

"Okay, we will check all that. Has your hair changed color since you were a kid?"

"I've been dyeing it since I was a teenager. And I also wear colored contact lenses."

Becker removed them from his eyes.

"I'm going to take them," Nico said.

The natural deep blue of Becker's eyes surprised Nico.

"I was determined to erase that child murderer forever, I guess. But that doesn't matter anymore, does it? Blue suits me better. I'll have to get used to it again."

"I'll need you to follow me to headquarters until we clear things up," Nico concluded, his hand unconsciously going to his stomach. It was a useless gesture, because only the treatment prescribed by Caroline would make it feel any better.

"You're not feeling well, are you?" Becker asked. "Didn't your doctor give you anything?"

"How do you know?"

"What? That you have an ulcer? Everyone knows. You yourself said that some information is hard to hide."

§ § §

She lived just yards away from Saint Germain des Prés, a neighborhood whose appeal dated back a century, when it was a haunt for writers and artists. The Place de Fürstenberg was her own little paradise. Her apartment was on the sixth and seventh floors of one of the buildings. It had a charming little terrace that overlooked the square and allowed her to enjoy the sun from one season to the next. She wouldn't have given it up for anything in the world.

She got undressed and stepped into the shower, relaxing under the hot water that massaged her shoulders and back. She was exhausted. Everything had happened so quickly over the last few days, and her stores of physical and mental energy were drained. She turned off the water with regret and wrapped herself in a soft terry bathrobe. She towel-dried her hair, then left the bathroom and fell onto the bed. She was hungry but didn't have the energy to make something to eat. She had to sleep. She would take care of the rest later. As soon as she made that decision, her eyes closed, and her breathing slowed. She lost consciousness and fell into a deep slumber.

§ § §

He had followed her. He had chosen her. She would be the next one. She looked so tired, and it would be easy. He was sure that she was already asleep. He admired the shop windows on the square. He had all the time he needed. Maybe he would even visit the Delacroix Museum; he had never had the opportunity to do so before. Then he would ring her doorbell. She would open it, annoyed at having been pulled out of her sleep. She wouldn't suspect anything, although she was central to the case. He would walk right through the door and into her apartment, and she would suffer the same punishment as the others. Nobody would be there to rescue her, and most of all, not Chief Sirsky.

§ § §

Magistrate Becker had followed Nico into his office. Michel Cohen had joined them, and the two police officers started the official questioning. Kriven's team was already reviewing his schedule for that week and had contacted his wife. They were getting a search warrant for his home. Professor Queneau would personally analyze Becker's DNA, as well as the colored contact lenses. The police machine was rolling. Dominique Kreiss was interviewing the educators and psychologists who had been responsible for Arnaud Briard until he was eighteen.

Could a boy who killed his mother in self-defense become a serial killer? If so, was he attacking his mother every time he killed a woman? Was this father of two, this loving husband really the culprit?

Nico thought about his son, the person he held dearest in the world. He would have to take him away from his mother for some time, which upset him more than he let show. Perhaps he would talk with a child psychiatrist to make sure Dimitri had all the emotional support he needed. He would ask Caroline for her professional opinion. She would know. Caroline—he wondered what she was doing at this moment. She had wanted to take a shower and rest a little, and would join him later. He would not let her go again. Tonight she would sleep at his place to be safe. He wanted her so much.

§ § §

She was so absorbed by her work that she started when her cell phone rang. It was Rémi. She hesitated and then decided to answer.

"Hey, sweetheart?"

"Yes," she said without much enthusiasm.

"Is something wrong?"

"No, everything is just fine."

"Will you be home late tonight?"

"I don't really know. I already told you, we're working on a complicated case."

"I know, but I wanted us to have a little tête-à-tête tonight."

"What do you mean by a little tête-à-tête?" she said with sarcasm.

"Why do you ask?"

"Do you mean a romantic dinner in a nice restaurant, holding my hand in the movies, going for a walk in the moonlight to talk about everything and nothing? No, none of that, of course. I know what a little tête-à-tête means to you. It means a good lay! And I've had enough."

"Enough of what? Enough of sex? You are such a prude."

"I'm not an object that exists just to satisfy your sexual fantasies, Rémi."

"You're all the same."

"What do you mean?"

"Nothing, forget it."

"You're right. I'm going to forget it. Or rather, I'm going to forget *you*. I'm fed up. I want something else from a relationship."

"Women are just not on the right wavelength."

"In any case, I am no longer on *your* wavelength."

"But you seemed to be having a good time. I thought you liked it."

"I do like it, but not under these conditions. Your saying that you want to go to bed isn't enough to get me excited."

"Foreplay—what bullshit!"

"Okay, pick up your things, and leave the keys in the mailbox."

"So it's over? Just like that?"

"Exactly. I want to move on, Rémi. Good luck."

"Bitch!"

"I want nothing more to do with you. I don't want to see you or hear from you again. Ciao."

Dominique slammed the phone down. She had wasted eight months, and that left a bitter taste in her mouth. Now she had to forget.

§ § §

He made sure the keyboard was inactive—he had no margin for error—then he slipped his cell phone into his inside jacket pocket. The time had come. He typed the code, and the door at 5 Place de Fürstenberg opened, as if by magic. He walked up five flights of stairs to reach his next victim's apartment. There was nobody to stop him. He was free to do as he pleased. He rang the bell. There was no reaction. He rang again. He put his ear against the door to listen and heard steps. He composed himself. She opened the door, her eyes still heavy with sleep.

"Yes, what is it?" she asked.

He did not give her any time to think. He jumped on her with all his force and covered her mouth. Very quickly, she turned into a rag doll in his arms. She was his. He was going to kill her. It would be like plunging a sword in Sirsky's heart.

SATURDAY

16

PERSONAL ATTACKS

His hands got lost in her wool sweater as he ran them up her back. Their mouths were sealed together. He pushed her onto the bed and lay on top of her. He kissed her stomach and slowly made his way to her neck. He pulled off her sweater, unbuttoned her shirt, and unhooked her bra. He brushed her chest and, descending to her hips, focused on removing her skirt. They smiled at each other and finished getting undressed. He threw himself on her again, unable to contain himself, tasting every inch of her skin and delaying the moment their bodies would join. The phone rang. It had to be a mistake. But the caller insisted, and it was difficult to ignore. A two-hour break was all that he wanted. They moved away from each other, burning with unappeased desire, their hearts pounding.

"Who is it?"

"Kriven, boss."

He wasn't his usual self. "What's going on?" Nico asked, suddenly worried.

"She's dead!" Commander Kriven sobbed.

"Who, for God's sake?"

"Amélie—Captain Ader! Her husband found her at home barely a half an hour ago."

"But how?" Nico asked, wanting to make sure that he had understood correctly.

"Like the others. The bastard really messed her up. It's horrible, Nico."

Kriven was crying now. "Shit! She could have been more careful!" he shouted. "She's a cop, damn it!"

"David, calm down. She couldn't be on guard twenty-four seven. Are you at the scene?"

"Yes. I haven't let anyone in. My team is outside, but I won't be able to control them for long. They want to see her. You understand."

"I'll be right there. Protect the scene. That's very important. I don't want anyone walking around Amélie's body."

"Okay, we'll wait for you. Hurry, Nico."

Kriven was begging him; he was on the brink of losing it. It was especially difficult to lose a colleague in the line of duty, and all the more so in such a horribly way. Nico wanted to scream. He had sent her home to get some rest. Guilt overwhelmed him. Amélie was talented and had a promising future. This case was becoming very personal. He wanted this asshole's blood, and he would get it.

He felt a warm hand on his shoulder. Caroline. He leaned into her for a few seconds to recharge his batteries.

"I have to go."

"A new victim?"

"Yes. From the team. A cop."

"Go quickly."

"Don't go anywhere, okay?"

"I'll stay here with Dimitri. Don't worry about us."

"Caroline?"

"Yes?"

"I really want you, you know…"

She smiled.

"I'll give you a rain check," she said with a wink.

Nico gave instructions to the two police officers assigned to protect Dimitri and Caroline and then got into his car.

He thought about the series of events. First, the mystery around Magistrate Becker. Jean-Marie Rost had uncovered nothing the judge's office, and Gamby hadn't found anything more on his computer. He and Cohen had led the search of his home personally but had come up with only a few old pictures. Alexandre Becker's past had been reduced to three or so modest shots of Arnaud Briard as a baby and young child, alone and with his mother. His wife was the only person who knew. She seemed kind and even-tempered. The sky had just fallen in on them. Her parents had come to pick up the two children, with Nico's consent; there was no reason to get them mixed up in this terrible story. Kriven's officers had examined the magistrate's schedule in detail. There were some gray areas; they had no way to verify the anonymous phone calls and the impromptu departures from his office. As a result, they had kept him in custody. And his former educators and psychologists couldn't contribute anything, other than saying that he had shown an exceptional ability to overcome the tragedy.

Nico, giving himself a break to see his son and Caroline, had left Becker no more than two hours earlier. Dimitri had arrived from his mother's place, with his things piled in suitcases. Sylvie had left without even waiting for Nico to get there. She had placed a sealed letter on the dresser in the entry. Her anxiety showed in the words, raising a number of questions about the future. She didn't say where she was going. She wanted to get help; she would return when she was better. She promised to keep in touch with Dimitri. She thanked Nico for his support and asked him not to try to find her; she needed to learn how to get by without him. That was key to her getting better.

Then Caroline had arrived under escort, as he had required. Her introduction to Dimitri could not have gone better. She had a good dose of psychology and knew how to handle teens. Dimitri wasn't fazed at all by this new person in his father's life and adopted her immediately. He clearly needed a strong and friendly female presence. Before Dimitri disappeared into his room, he gave them a smile that warmed Nico's heart. After that, Nico had only one thing on his mind: getting Caroline into his bed. They flirted for a few minutes, and then they threw themselves at each other, unable to hold back any longer. Until Kriven called about the murder of his second in command, Captain Amélie Ader.

Nico arrived at the Place de Fürstenberg. The flashing blue and yellow lights of the police cars illuminated the building. The feverish activity at this hour of the morning had awakened the neighbors. Captain Pierre Vidal was smoking a cigarette. Everyone knew he had stopped smoking nearly two years earlier. The news had been too much. The other squad members stood near him, still and silent. Théron's men were there too.

A car was let through the roadblock that had been set up around the square. Cohen got out, accompanied by Nicole Monthalet herself. The presence of the police commissioner did not go unnoticed. She shook hands and said a few words of comfort. She was one with this family: the police. Nico appreciated her presence. Together, they climbed the stairs to Captain Ader's apartment. Pierre Vidal followed, ready to get to work as soon as the order was given. Nico had suggested that he let someone else take over, because he had worked with Amélie every day, but he refused. Rost and Kriven were waiting for them; Maxime Ader was next to them. Nico knew him from La Crim' get-togethers. He was trying to hold himself together.

"Amélie is in the living room," Commander Kriven said, his voice filled with emotion.

The sight of Amélie's nude and mutilated body was a nightmare. It was the madness of a man who had lost all trace of humanity.

"I didn't touch anything," Maxime Ader said.

"There's another message," Nicole Monthalet said, pointing to an envelope on the victim's thigh. She put on the gloves that Captain Vidal handed her and took the letter. Inside, there was a carefully folded piece of paper and two handwritten sentences.

"Can't you even protect your women, Nico? I am God. You are nothing," Madame Monthalet read.

"The bastard!" Cohen shrieked.

"One thing now seems obvious," Nico said. "Becker is innocent. I sent Amélie home when I went to the magistrate's office. He hasn't been alone since. We no longer have to keep him in custody."

Three custody rooms were next to his office. He had put Magistrate Becker in one of them and had left him sitting on a narrow bench, guarded by two uniformed officers, as regulations required. Nico had no choice. He had to lock Becker up until he was cleared. He had seen the magistrate's crestfallen look at finding himself there, confined within the graffiti-covered walls, but Nico could not allow himself to feel pity. Now he was relieved to let him go. It was reassuring to see that Becker had, in fact, overcome his childhood trauma. They needed to start the investigation fresh.

"Let's get going. Search the scene," Nico ordered. "And we have to get Amélie out of here. Has someone told Professor Vilars?"

"Yes," Rost answered. "She is already at the medical examiner's office."

"Very good. Jean-Marie, you take care of the body," Nico said.

Everyone went to work, under the seasoned eye of Nicole Monthalet. When Amélie Ader's body was carried through the apartment in a body bag, they all stopped what they were doing and watched in respectful silence. Maxime Ader, tears streaming down his face, decided to go with his wife.

"I've got an ear print on the door!" Captain Vidal's voice rang out.

Nico approached.

"Maybe our man listened before he rang," Vidal said.

The lifted ear print would be compared to the culprit's when the time came, and this would be one more piece of evidence against him.

"There's a white powder on the dining room table," Nicole Monthalet said. "Come take a look, Chief Sirsky."

"It might be talc," Nico said. "He uses surgical gloves. The talc scatters when he opens the sterile package."

Quickly they realized that they wouldn't find anything else. The killer had kept a cool head and made only a few mistakes. It was enraging. Monthalet and Cohen decided to go to the medical examiner's office to attend the autopsy. Nico forbade his men to follow, despite how unhappy that clearly made Kriven. It was out of the question that they watch their colleague go under the coroner's scalpel.

On the way back to headquarters, Nico obsessed over the killer's latest message. The discomfort was palpable when Nicole Monthalet read it. "Can't you even protect your women, Nico? I am God. You are nothing." The scumbag was blaming him. Why had he forced Amélie to go home? Why hadn't he let her continue her work at headquarters, as she had wanted to? Was it to reward her for discovering the link to Magistrate Becker? Was it because they badly needed rested, available detectives? Or was it because she was a woman, and he was treating her differently, as she had suggested? Undoubtedly, it was all of these reasons. His decision had led to her death.

How terribly ironic—to be tortured by the very person he was tracking. Nico needed to bring down this criminal. But what exactly did he mean by "your women"? Was the killer telling him clearly that other women who were even closer to him were also in danger? The idea sent a shiver up his spine. Who was next on the list? His head was buzzing with questions when he arrived at headquarters. He double parked, leaving the key in the ignition, under the watchful eye of some uniformed officers. He went directly to the custody room where Magistrate Becker was being held.

The man had been sitting on the same bench for several hours. His face was in his hands. Nico relieved the officers and opened the glass door.

"You are free to go," he said.

"That means that something must have happened, right? A murder while I was in custody? That's abominable. I am so sorry for the poor woman."

Becker didn't stand up to leave, but instead continued to sit on the bench. Nico sat down beside him. The two men remained silent for several minutes.

"The woman in question, the killer's fifth victim, was a member of my team," Nico finally said.

"A cop?"

"Captain Amélie Ader. She's the one who made the connection between you and Arnaud Briard."

"She did good work."

"Exactly. But it was a lead in the wrong direction. I sent her home to get some rest after she made the discovery. And she was killed."

"It's not your fault," Becker said, as if he were reading his thoughts.

"So it seems."

"A new message?"

"Yes. 'Can't you even protect your women, Nico? I am God. You are nothing.'"

"This determination of his to undermine you reveals a real sense of inferiority."

"Is he being sarcastic, or is it a threat?"

"You're wondering if *your women* could be in danger?"

"You could say that."

"Is your family still under police protection?"

"Yes."

"Is this personal, or does he want to destroy you because you are the head of the Criminal Investigation Division?"

"We didn't find anything when we looked into the people I've put away in recent years."

"We have a real sociopath on our hands. He's well integrated. He's employed, and apparently, he has, no prior record. The day you put someone like that behind bars, he never gets out again. But why did he bring up my past? How did he know?"

"He did it to mislead us and keep us off his trail."

"You, me—"

"That said, maybe he is not so far removed from us."

"You're giving me goose bumps."

"Amélie Ader's autopsy has certainly begun. Are you coming?"

"I have to reassure my wife."

"It's been done already. I called her just a few minutes ago. I warned her that you would have work to do and wouldn't be coming home right away."

"What attention to detail. Thanks. I'm right behind you, Nico. I can call you Nico, can't I?"

"With pleasure. We're going to have to start from square one again."

"I'm with you. After the autopsy, get the whole team together in your office."

"Okay. We need to find him before he kills again. There has to be something we missed."

"And at Ader's place?"

"Similar ropes around her wrists. The talc and an ear print on the front door."

"That's not much. The SOB is careful."

"Or he knows our methods."

"Today anybody can know them just by watching TV and reading mysteries."

"Not in such detail."

"Perhaps not, but everyone knows not to leave evidence and fingerprints and that DNA is a key part of any investigation."

"He knows how to stitch up skin and where to get surgical sutures. You don't know that from just watching a show or reading a book."

"Touché."

The men stood up. They left police headquarters and got into the chief's car to go to the medical examiner's office.

"You have a son, don't you?" Becker asked.

"Yes. Dimitri. He's fourteen years old."

"So you're married?"

"Divorced. It's been awhile. Someone else came into my life recently."

"Are you in love?"

"Crazy in love."

Nico parked his car in front of the Institut Médico-Légal. The two men entered the building and were greeted by the guard. They walked to the autopsy room, ready to brace themselves against the chill required by the nature of the clientele.

"Hello, Nico," said Professor Vilars, who was leaning over the victim's body and had clearly made progress. "I'm sorry for Ader."

"Thanks."

"*Monsieur le Juge*," she added in a respectful tone, indicating that she was relieved to see him with the chief.

"I am glad to see that everything has been cleared up and that you have joined us," Nicole Monthalet said, holding out her hand for a firm shake.

"I am, as well," Michel Cohen said in turn.

"Do you have anything?" Nico asked, looking at Professor Vilars.

"You're not going to like this," her assistant, Eric Fiori, said.

"First of all, once again there were thirty whip lashes," Armelle added as she dissected the victim's organs.

Nico had to turn away from the police captain's stiff body, which had incisions from top to bottom. He gave Armelle Vilars a worried look. She would guess his despair, but she wouldn't say anything in front of his superiors, especially not in front of Nicole Monthalet. Nico tried to swallow, but he had a knot in his throat.

"Examination of the body didn't yield any promising leads, aside from traces of talc on her ankles. He must have squeezed them tight, because there is bruising."

"She must have been kicking very hard," Madame Monthalet said. "He wanted to hold her down."

"That's likely. I will continue, if you don't mind," Professor Vilars said. "Are you sure that you're okay?"

They all knew the victim, which, under normal circumstances, would be sufficient reason to ban them from the autopsy. Armelle had never broken this rule before, and she didn't like the idea of doing it now. By staying, their minds would record images that would remain with them their entire lives.

"Nico, you worked with her every day," Cohen said. "You should leave."

"I'm staying. No question."

"Cohen is right. You don't have to be a hero, Chief Sirsky," Nicole Monthalet said. "We know how thoroughly capable you are and how important you are to our organization. Your presence here serves no purpose. We understand."

"Listen, I know what I'm doing. It's my job to be here."

"Damn it!" Professor Vilars let out, surprising everyone. "What are you trying to prove, Nico? Now get out. I don't want you here. I don't want anyone here who was Captain Ader's colleague. Is that understood? You will have my report in two hours. Now enough. I've seen enough of you."

"She's right," Becker said, trying to appease Nico. "Go on. I'll see you in your office as soon as this is over. Mr. Cohen will take me back to headquarters."

"Fine. I see everyone is against me."

"You will thank us later," Armelle said, and then she winked at him.

17

COMMON FRONT

He had gotten to him where it hurt. He had caused him to despair. He had struck him with full force and had shaken up the man who thought of himself as stronger and more clever than everyone else. Nico Sirsky, chief of the famous Paris Criminal Investigation division, was losing his bearings. Soon both legs would buckle, and he would eat dust. Just as his mother had.

§ § §

Nico arrived at headquarters. He had an overwhelming desire to hear Caroline's voice, but he didn't dare call her. He simply imagined her smile, the one that had changed his life. Maybe she was sleeping under the comforter in his bed. Deep down, all he wanted was to listen to her regular breathing, to lie next to her, and to get lost in her smell. Most of all, he wanted to take up the conversation where he had left off, in her arms.

He went through the checkpoint guarded by two uniformed officers. One of them had raised his voice at a man Nico didn't know. He heard Dominique Kreiss's name, but he decided not to get involved. He climbed the stairs to the offices. The lights were so intense, it almost seemed like daytime. The sound of voices assailed him. He understood that his men were there, that none of them had been able to go home after the night's macabre discovery. He walked toward the offices assigned to Kriven's men. When he entered, faces turned to him, and everyone became quiet. They were all there—Kriven's and Théron's teams, along with their superior officer, Deputy Chief Rost. Dominique Kreiss was also there; her eyes were red. They had spread the word, and everyone had rushed to the offices.

"He killed Ader. Nobody can do anything about that," Nico said. "Five victims, and it won't end unless we arrest him. So we are going to start from square one again and burn rubber. I want him dead or alive. I think we all agree, don't we?"

They all nodded.

"Kriven, I want you and your team to follow the Triflex lead," Nico continued. "That's the brand of surgical gloves the killer is using. I want to know who produces them, who distributes them, and where they go in Paris. It's a common product, but I don't give a shit. It might get us a lead. Théron? Go back to the nautical rope. I know the man probably bought it anonymously with cash. Still, go back over the retailers' customers. Would the killer buy this type of rope if he didn't like boating? Would you have bought it? Of course not; like me, you would have used nylon rope from the supermarket, the usual kind."

"Maybe he knew about your brother-in-law's passion for sailing," Théron said. "So using that type of rope would throw suspicion on a member of your family."

"That is possible. Rost! How is Walberg doing on the handwriting analysis of the last message?"

"He'll be here with his report any minute," Rost responded. "The lab is going to call about the ear print we found on Amélie's door and about the rope used this time."

"Did the bastard amputate Amélie's breasts as he did with the others?" an officer from Kriven's group asked.

"Yes," Nico said.

"Was she pregnant?" Kriven asked.

"I don't know yet. The autopsy wasn't finished when they threw me out."

"It's better that way," Rost said. "None of us could have stood seeing such a thing. It's Amélie, after all."

"The first four victims were a month pregnant," Nico said. "How does he get that information?"

"Gamby says it's easy for the killer to hack into the computers of certain practitioners and medical laboratories," Kriven said.

"Okay. But they had appointments with their doctors only a few days before being killed," said Théron. "That wouldn't give him much time to plan his crimes. Yet he knows his victims' habits well. For example, he knew that Marie-Hélène Jory did not work on Monday mornings and that Valérie Trajan took Wednesday off. Nurses have hours that change from one week to the next. It would have been very hard to know what time Isabelle Saulière was going off duty on Thursday. And what about Ader? That was impossible to plan."

"That's true," Nico said. "I'm the one who sent her home to rest. She did a good job and deserved it. If I hadn't given her the order, she would have stayed here."

The room went quiet.

"What if we are wrong, and he knew them all?" Nico finally said.

Kriven reacted. "What do you mean?"

"Someone you confide in about being pregnant even before telling your husband or your mother?" Dominique Kreiss asked.

"Why not? Rost, I want you to lead the search. We need to get the victims' phones and look at their contact lists again. Question their friends and families and compare."

"Okay."

"And then there are the messages he is leaving," Nico said.

"Messages with biblical connotations that are meant specifically for you," Dominique Kreiss said.

"In the latest, he talked about protecting your women; was he referring to Amélie?" Kriven asked.

"I think so," the psychologist said. "But he might be threatening other women Nico knows with the clear goal that he 'not be able to rise' on Sunday. It is possible that he will target someone who means a lot to you, Nico, making the last murder an apotheosis."

"A sociopath cannot put an end to his criminal activity by simply deciding to do so," Nico reacted. "Killing is an absolute necessity for him."

"He can put an end to a series of murders, as if he has won a round," Dominique said. "He will kill again, elsewhere, differently. But he will have conquered the chief of police and no longer be a nobody."

"I don't understand why he would use Nico's medical file," Rost said. "And how did he know that you had an appointment at Saint Antoine Hospital?"

"I didn't talk to anyone about it, except my family. My brother-in-law made the appointment for me."

"Could it be a friend or acquaintance of a family member?" Rost asked. "Between your brother-in-law's love of the sea and your medical file, it seems our man has some very personal information about you."

"I think you should check it out," Kriven said.

"Fine," Nico admitted. "Get to work. Breakfast with those in charge in my office at eight. That gives you more than four hours. Wake up every available man. Another murder is scheduled in a few hours. Let's not forget that. Dominique, can I talk to you for a second?"

"Of course."

"I heard some guy asking after you outside when I arrived earlier. It was three in the morning."

"Oh, that's Rémi."

"Rémi? He didn't seem very easy to get along with."

"I ended it with him yesterday. We'd been together for eight months."

"I'm sorry to hear that."

"It's my problem," the psychologist said, stiffening.

Nico was on slippery ground, talking about a colleague's private life. It was not his habit to get involved in the personal lives of those he worked with, but Dominique's ex had shown up at headquarters. He wanted to make sure it wouldn't go any further, and she had everything under control.

"You're sure that it will be okay? He's not going to make life difficult for you?"

"He has an aggressive personality. To tell the truth, other than the sex, I wonder what it is that he likes about women. I told the officers downstairs that I didn't want to see him, and they sent him away."

"He'll come back, either here or at your place."

"I know."

"You are sure I have nothing to worry about?"

"Nothing at all. I will take care of this, like a big girl."

"Don't hesitate to talk to me if things get out of hand."

"Promise."

Dominique Kreiss went to join the others. Nico dived into his teams' reports. He paid special attention to the memos from the counter-terrorism section, because it was important to remain alert to the risk of attack. International relations supplied multiple motives for terrorism in France.

Someone knocked at the door. He looked up and invited Marc Walberg to come in. "I wanted to come to see you," he said. "It was on my way."

"Do you have something new?"

"For the first time I have a document of real interest, because the killer wrote on paper and not on a mirror or a door. The paper provides key information with its patterns, watermark, weight, dimensions, thickness, grain, color, and light sensitivity. With these, we can identify the exact brand and type of paper, which can lead us to the person who sold it. I have the address right here. Paper is also malleable, which means that when something presses against it, it leaves a mark. We generally examine the paper under a microscope, because the impression is often barely visible. I once discerned the brand on a jacket button and the type of material on a chair from examining a piece of paper under a microscope. Now, on this piece of paper, I've found an impression."

"Yes?"

"A signature. The killer must have used a piece of paper that was originally underneath another piece of paper used for something else. Perhaps they were pages from a pad of paper. The killer's paper picked up the impression of the signature. The writing is not the same as our man's. I'm absolutely sure about that. Unfortunately, the signature is more of a scribble than a legible name. I magnified it here."

Nico contemplated this piece of evidence.

"Although I didn't find any fingerprints, the handwriting analysis was interesting. When I examined the first message, I told you that the person who wrote it knew exactly what he was doing. Then he started showing signs of nervousness, which changed his writing. Finally, remember that he attempted to disguise the writing by making it more feminine. In this last message, I spotted a number of inconsistencies linked to the feminization and signs of intense stress."

"Stress?"

"Yes, this time, our man hesitated when he wrote the message and wasn't able to control his shaking."

"That contradicts what he wrote."

"True, but that doesn't mean anything. By challenging you, the killer has become engaged in a power struggle that makes him more vulnerable. So there you have everything I know."

"Thank you, Marc. Good work."

"I hope that it helps you catch him. Don't hesitate to call me at any hour. I know how serious this case is."

The forensic specialist left, probably to return to the warmth of his home. Nico called Kriven.

"David, I have another mission for your team. Walberg found the brand of paper the criminal used and the supplier. I want you to make contact. Find out what customers they have in Paris. We need to compare that with the Triflex distribution network."

"Consider it done. Who are they?"

Nico gave him the name and contact information and hung up. A heavy silence settled in the office. He grabbed his cell phone from his jacket pocket. He weighed it in his hand for a second; he hesitated. He had to talk to her. The need was so strong. He called his home phone, running the risk of waking both her and his son. The phone rang once, and she picked it up.

"Caroline?"

"Yes."

"Is everything all right?"

"Fine. Dimitri is sleeping like a baby. I thought you might call."

"I wanted to hear your voice. I miss you."

He could hear her smile.

"Where are you?" he asked.

"In your bed, I'm reading some magazines. Have you made any progress in the investigation?"

"Perhaps."

"You'll keep me posted, won't you?"

"Of course. In any case, don't leave the house."

"Understood."

"Caroline?"

"Yes?"

"I love you."

"Nico!"

"Talk to you later."

Kriven rushed in without knocking. Nico ended the call.

"She's a bomb," David Kriven said.

"Who's that?"

"Sorry, I overheard. Caroline Dalry of course. I'm impressed. And she's a doctor on top of that!"

"Commander Kriven, please control yourself."

"I'm just saying I think she's a good catch. She has something special. I mean, uh, a lot of charm."

"I know. Okay, it's not teatime. Do you have something interesting to tell me?"

"Triflex belongs to an American company, Allegiance Healthcare Corporation. The product is produced in Thailand. There is a subsidiary in Brittany, in Châteaubriant. The local police chief went to wake up the manager. We'll have the list of Paris customers shortly."

"Perfect. And the paper?"

"We're working on it. I'll tell you later. I had Maxime Ader on the phone. He is waiting at the morgue until the autopsy is over. Professor Vilars will see him right after she's finished."

"I hope he is not alone."

"No. He has family with him. There's a whole pack of them. The funeral will probably take place at the beginning of the week. The police benevolent association could do a collection to help out, what do you think?"

"That's a good idea," Nico said.

He took out his wallet and found a hundred-euro bill, which he held out to his commander. Kriven appreciated his boss's gesture.

§ § §

He had come close to Nico Sirsky. The jubilation he felt was unforgettable. The chief was upset. That was obvious. He couldn't stop this series of murders. All he could do was observe the damage: the bodies of these innocent women, tortured and murdered. And the most recent one was a cop. How ironic! The great chief could not protect his own and was not, in reality, as brilliant as everyone said. He was going to fall off his pedestal. If only Sirsky knew that they had brushed against each other, that their skin had touched! Nico was good at everything, but he was going to lose the most important thing he had. He knew which woman to attack. Sirsky would never again be the same man. He would no longer have a taste for life. He would descend into hell.

§ § §

Armelle had just finished the autopsy. It would take her some time to relax her mind and body. As usual, she had worked with meticulous detail, leaning over the body, reducing it to a complex and fascinating object of her expertise. Her job was to find a cause of death, and it was the very reason she championed life. Of course, the lives of those who arrived here had been abruptly interrupted by a crime or an accident. It was up to her to explain why and how. Up to her to uncover death's mysteries. And there were the families. Her sense of moral duty required her to give them her special attention. The living who ended up here probably never imagined one day setting foot in the Institut Médico-Légal; they were disoriented by the place, shattered by the loss of their loved ones. So they turned to her, hoping for explanations and support. She listened, and to calm the rage and pain, she weighed every word she said so they could begin grieving under the best possible conditions.

Many sordid stories inhabited her memory; she wasn't able to wave a magic wand and make them disappear. They were all part of her. Could anyone imagine that dissecting Captain Ader's body was just another autopsy? She had met the woman on several occasions when she had attended autopsies, like all the other detectives. Vilars was good at remembering faces and had a precise image of her in her mind. Amélie Ader loved her job. She still had that freshness and energy that came with youth, despite the dire realities of her work. Now she was nothing more than a lifeless body mutilated by a killer and an autopsy. The medical examiner's job required a rare strength of character; she had to have the energy to defy death every day.

She made a quick stop in her office before going to see the Ader family. First, she had to contact Sirsky. Of course, his superiors and Magistrate Becker would tell him exactly what happened during the autopsy, but she wanted to talk to him personally. That, too, was her duty; the specific nature of the situation required it. The chief inspector answered her call immediately.

"I'm finished," she said. "Your team is on its way back."

"Thank you, Armelle. I know that it couldn't have been easy for you."

He always had that same sensitivity. His reactions never ceased to surprise her. "I'll manage," she said, not wanting to say any more about it. "I wanted to warn you. I found some interesting elements."

"Like what?"

"Overall, the scenario was the same. We are dealing with the same murderer. There is one major difference, however. Amélie Ader was not pregnant. The breasts sewn onto her thorax were those of the previous victim, Isabelle Saulière. The tests will prove that without a doubt. Now, to the heart of the matter. I used a UV light. You know that many biological substances become fluorescent in certain light. Then I did it again, using luminol, which is a chemical that highlights even the tiniest biological trace. Well, our man licked the victim's breasts. He left saliva on them and, therefore, DNA. We are testing it now."

"Well, well, he finally made a mistake."

"Except that you have to wait twenty-four hours to have the first results. Professor Queneau is doing the best he can, but he cannot do the test any faster."

"That's too long, I fear. We need to be faster than that if we want to prevent a sixth slaying."

"I have more. I found the imprint of a shoe on the victim's skull. He fractured the right parietal bone and part of the frontal. He used his full weight, because the footprint is perfectly identifiable. And I removed a substance that was most probably left there by the shoe. I'm going to analyze it. I'll call you back as quickly as possible to tell you what it is."

"What do you think it is?"

"A plant perhaps. Give me some time to look at it under a microscope. I have just gotten my botanical specialist up. He's on his way."

"Good job, Armelle."

"Forensics is an art, Nico, not an exact science. I don't repair people or save them. I observe them to explain how they died. I find clues. That's my job. I'll be happy if I can provide a report that helps your investigation."

Armelle Vilars hung up. She took a deep breath and entered the room reserved for families. Amélie Ader's loved ones were waiting. They were looking for explanations. They wanted to know if she had suffered. Experience had taught her that she shouldn't hide any information from the people who wanted to know everything about the death; she would tell them the tiniest, most horrible details if that was what they needed. She had been trained to control her emotions.

18

THE CHASE

It was eight in the morning. A map of Paris was spread on Nico's worktable. Red markers showed the victims' addresses. The list of places that had the Triflex surgical gloves and the paper used by the criminal hung on an office wall. The crossovers were highlighted in yellow. There were several of them, including hospitals, labs, medical offices, and veterinary clinics.

"The two companies supply Saint Antoine Hospital," Magistrate Becker said.

"But where does that lead us?" Nico said.

§ § §

Erwan Kellec was a renowned botanical specialist with advanced knowledge in phanerogams. Seed plants—whether they were ginkgoes, conifers, or flowering plants—held no secrets for him. He worked in the National Natural History Museum on the Rue Buffon, and helped the medical examiner with identification when needed. As soon as Armelle pulled him out of his bed and explained the situation, he had gone straight to work. He loved the feeling of adventure and excitement and had rushed in to examine the small amounts of plant matter that Professor Vilars had collected.

"And so?" Nico asked with some impatience.

"Catchfly," Armelle said into the phone. "That's one of its common names. It's also known as red campion."

"Sorry, this is beyond my realm of expertise," Nico said.

"*Silene dioica* is the scientific name. It's in the *Caryophyllaceae* family. *Dioica* means that it has male and female flowers. The female flowers have no stamens, but the males have ten. Male plants are most common in gardens. They have limp stems with a ramification on the top, and the leaves are broad, oval, and pointed. Flowering occurs from May to September. The pink petals are divided. This plant species is considered relatively rare in the region."

§ § §

They would soon discover his identity. He was still eluding them, but he could feel the noose tightening. He couldn't deny their skill and know-how, even if he had left them a few clues. All they had to do was bring together all the elements they had in hand, analyze them, and compare the information, and the truth would come out. He had hesitated before choosing the best strategy. He would have preferred killing *her*. What a pleasure it would have been to see the horror and death in her eyes. He would have savored the irony of all of them standing around her cold body spread out on a table, the masked faces leaning over her, the gloved hands holding rib shears and opening her thorax. Perhaps he could have done this himself, carrying out the motions that she had done a thousand times—the gestures that she so often said she wished she didn't have to make. He would have loved seeing her suffer. She deserved it. That woman he wanted but never managed to possess. He was undoubtedly not

good enough for her. They had never seen the superior
creature that he really was, the all-powerful man that
he was. But he had to focus on his goal: Nico Sirsky.
Armelle would be spared. He had another mission. And
God would help him carry it out. He was God.

§ § §

As the day began in the capital, the investigators continued their work in the field. They targeted all Triflex users
who also ordered 80-gram Copa Plus A4 white paper.
They questioned friends of the victims about the people
they knew and searched through their personal things for
some overlooked piece of evidence. Nico gathered all the
information together, hoping that a serious lead would
spring from all this commotion.

At ten in the morning Nico stood in front of the lists
pinned to his office wall. Becker was next to him. There
had to be a solution. Maybe it was there, in front of them,
and they just hadn't seen it. Was it too obvious? The
phone rang for the nth time. Nico grabbed it.

"It's Armelle here. There's something that caught my
attention. You know, I'm very familiar with those red
campions. Several years ago, I had a garden planted at
the medical examiner's complex. The windows of my office look out onto it. Gardening relaxes me at home, and
believe me, looking at that garden at work does me a lot
of good. It is a beautiful enclosed plot with a fountain,
and it's open to all the personnel here. When the garden
was planted, I wanted several red campion specimens,
because the flowers are really beautiful. To make a long
story short, I was just out there. Our discovery made me

want to take a look at the plants up close, and, well, it's stupid, but…"

"What's stupid, Armelle?" Nico asked, his voice tense.

"Well, my red campions, my favorite flowers in the garden, um, they were trampled. Can you imagine that? It's incredible."

"Yes, it is incredible."

"And, well, you can't find those plants just anywhere."

"What are you trying to say, Armelle?"

"I don't know. When I saw those very plants ruined, it sent a shiver up my spine."

"What is your conclusion?"

"What if I compare samples?"

"Those we found on Captain Ader's body with the red campions in your garden?"

"That's right."

Nico was speechless and thinking quickly.

"Nico?" Armelle said, sounding worried.

"I'll be right there."

§ § §

It was eleven. The car was there, parked along the sidewalk, a few yards from the double doors that led to the private alley. Two uniformed security officers were staying warm in the car. From time to time, one of them would leave the vehicle, pace up and down the street, and then type in the gate code allowing access to the houses. He would look around, making sure there was nothing out of the ordinary, and then return to the car. Easy. He already had a plan to outsmart them. They couldn't do anything to stop him; he was invincible. He would sweep down on his next victim: the seventh woman.

§ § §

Nico and Alexandre stared at the trampled garden in the medical examiner's complex. It couldn't be a coincidence. Clearly someone had wanted to crush Professor Vilars's flowers.

"Kellec is sure about it. The samples collected from the victim come from this spot," Armelle confirmed.

"And you use Triflex gloves in the autopsy room, don't you?" Nico asked.

Armelle nodded.

"In addition, the paper you have delivered here is the same as what the killer used to write his message," Magistrate Becker continued.

"Do you know whose signature this is?" Nico asked, holding out a close-up picture.

The coroner's eyes widened. Alarmed, she swallowed hard.

"It's mine!"

"That incomprehensible scribbling?" Nico asked.

"It's the signature I use for everyday documents and internal memos. I have a more legible one for correspondence that leaves the institute."

"We need to take a closer look at your employees."

"My employees?"

"That's right, Armelle. Have you noticed anything unusual lately? Any problems with a colleague?"

Taken aback, she knit her brow. She felt her stomach tighten with anxiety. Nico sensed it and put a hand on her shoulder, trying to reassure her.

§ § §

Tanya had had enough of being locked up inside; the kids were stir-crazy, and her mother was getting on her nerves with all of her fretting over Nico and Dimitri. Her husband's usual color was returning little by little, but he was having trouble moving on; it was as though he had been run over by a semi. In short, she felt like grabbing her husband and mother and giving them a good shake, but she knew it would be better to just take a walk and get some air. The question was how to get by the policemen guarding the building. She decided not to say anything and to just leave, letting the television cover the sound of her exit. She could always ask the concierge to distract the police while she climbed out the ground-floor window. She could manage that. A short walk, and nobody would know she was gone. At worst, she'd have to get Nico to forgive her. He wouldn't hold it against her. He adored her. And he owed her one for introducing him to Caroline.

§ § §

She was pretty and alluring, a good catch for his father. It was about time. He hoped it would work out. Furthermore, she would make a perfect stepmother. She had helped him finish his math homework and was now correcting his French composition. Clearly, she didn't have trouble with any subjects, and she knew how to teach. He already enjoyed her voice and liked listening to her. She was nothing like his always-nervous mother. He was getting attached to this reassuring female presence. He would have loved it if Sylvie were like that.

§ § §

Armelle cleared her throat.

"Um. Yes, Eric Fiori has seemed a little tense lately. I've had words with him several times."

"Where is he?" Nico asked.

"He went home."

"When?"

Armelle thought for an instant. "After I discovered the trace of red campion on the victim's scull."

"What state of mind was he in?"

"It's hard to say. I was busy working at the time. But in the past few days, he has been kind of aggressive."

"Where does he live?" Becker asked.

"Let's go in, and I'll find his address."

Becker wanted to know how long he had worked there.

"Four years."

"Never any problems?" Nico asked.

"On occasion he has been forward with me, but each time I've put him in his place. He's not the easiest member of the team to get along with, but he's a good pathologist. Here's where he lives."

"Can we see his office?"

"Of course. Follow me."

On the way, Nico called Deputy Chief Rost and asked him to stake out Eric Fiori's home.

§ § §

It hadn't been hard to convince the concierge. Tanya walked away from her home with an intoxicating feeling of freedom. The police in charge of her safety hadn't noticed anything. She was already imagining how angry her brother would be if he discovered that she had gone out on her own. With a little luck, he wouldn't know, and nobody would get in trouble. Her family thought she was closed up in her office, and she had insisted that she not be bothered. She had drawings to finish for her architecture firm. It was true, but her heart was not in her work. Breathing in the exhaust fumes and other odors of the capital was exactly what she needed. She stopped at a stall in front of a shop and admired the magnificent fruit. She couldn't resist and did some shopping for lunch. She regretted having to go back before anyone noticed her absence. She caught a glimpse of a man who was staring at her, shamelessly devouring her with his eyes. It happened to her all the time. She tried not to give him any attention and continued on her way. Imperceptibly, she started walking faster—and was even becoming sorry about her escapade—until someone ran into her. Some oranges rolled onto the sidewalk. He bent over and picked them up. It was the same man, the one who had been staring at her, and he insisted.

§ § §

Eric Fiori's office was a perfect example of cleanliness and order. Not a single paper was out of place; there wasn't even a pen without a cap. Nico began searching, opening the drawers, one by one. His face went serious, and he held out a cardboard box to show Becker.

"Contact lenses," Nico said.

Alexandre Becker read what was on the box. "Contact lenses +4.00 for hyperopia," he said.

"I'll take a few notes written by Dr. Fiori so that Marc Walberg can compare the handwriting," Nico said. "I don't see anything else of interest here."

"I have something of interest," Becker said.

"What's that?"

"It was Eric Fiori who told me about your health concerns."

"Fiori? But I barely know this guy, and I never told him anything about it."

"He knew, though. He knew that you had a stomachache and that you had had an endoscopy at Saint Antoine Hospital."

"But I didn't tell anyone. He couldn't have known."

"Somebody must have known."

"There were only three people, and they are family members. Alexis Perrin made the appointment for me, and then there were my sister and my mother. That's all."

"But someone told him."

"It is totally impossible!"

Nico grabbed his cell phone and called Tanya's number. His brother-in-law answered.

"Hey, does the name Eric Fiori mean anything to you?"

"Nothing at all."

"*Dr.* Fiori, perhaps?"

"No, nothing."

"Can you put Tanya on?"

"I'll go get her. She's in her office. She's catching up on her work. You have to admit that things have been a little disorganized recently. Here, wait a minute. Tanya? Tanya? That's strange. She's not answering."

"She can't be far."

"Wait a second. Tanya? Damn it, she's gone."

"I don't see her anywhere," said Anya. "Where is she?"

"Nico?" Alexis said in a worried voice. "She's gone."

"What the hell is going on? She didn't just take off, did she?"

"She doesn't like to be pent up," Alexis said. "You know your sister. She always has to do exactly what she wants."

"I'm hanging up and contacting the policemen in front of your building."

§ § §

The impression of being undressed by his eyes sent a shiver up her spine, like the feel of his breath on her neck. He handed her the oranges and smiled at her. She didn't like his expression. He was a handsome man, but she found everything about him repulsive. She was in a hurry to get home.

§ § §

She was so close to him. The time had come to complete his work. Afterward, it didn't really matter what happened to him, because he would have won. Nico Sirsky would never forget him. In a way, he would have succeeded in his quest for immortality. He had twenty-four hours in front of him, and he was going to spend them with her.

§ § §

Nico gave them an earful they would remember for a long time. Until Tanya came around the corner and joined them. The two police officers looked chastened. She apologized to her brother, explaining that the two uniforms had done nothing wrong.

"You deserve a good spanking!" Nico said. "Do you really think this is a good time to do stupid things? We'll talk about this later."

"Okay, okay. I'm sorry. I wasn't being very responsible. I'm aware of that. But I'm here now, aren't I? Let's move on."

"Exactly. I want to know if you're familiar with a man named Eric Fiori, Dr. Fiori."

"Eric? Of course. Why?"

"What do you mean 'of course'? Your husband has no idea who he is."

"Oh, that's not surprising. I know him from the gym, from the weight room and squash. We've even played together."

"How long have you known him?"

"I don't know, maybe three or four months."

"Did you talk to him about me?"

"About you? Why in the world—"

"Because he knew I had an appointment at Saint Antoine Hospital, that's why."

"Oh. It's possible I told him."

"Possible?"

"You know what it's like. It was a conversation."

"With someone you don't know? And you go and tell him about your brother's health issues?"

"But he's a doctor. I just asked him what he thought."

"And do you know what kind of doctor he is?"

"What kind? I don't know. A doctor is a doctor. Who cares what his specialty is? I only see him from time to time."

"Enough for you to tell him all about your private life."

"Stop it, Nico. You're exaggerating."

"I've got news for you. Eric Fiori is a coroner. His patients are kind of stiff, if you get my meaning. Does that make a difference?"

Tanya went pale.

"And he may just be the serial killer I'm looking for," Nico added.

§ § §

The moment was exhilarating. It was a few seconds of pure happiness. There he was, standing in Chief Sirsky's dining room, his pistol digging into the back of the uniformed officer in charge of guarding the house. He had waited until one of the two cops entered the private alleyway that led to Sirsky's home and had followed him. Nothing could have been easier. There was a day-care center at the same address. He acted like a good family man and carried a child's sweater. He wore a happy smile and approached. Then all he had to do was point the gun at the policeman. Dr. Dalry was now glaring at him. He would have expected more fear, but no, she showed self-assurance. The teenager was clearly shocked. He had to be Sirsky's son; the resemblance was striking. Caroline Dalry had put a protective hand on his shoulder. Soon, she wouldn't be so smooth. She would beg him, like the others.

"Do you know who I am?" he asked her.

"Not yet," she answered calmly.

"Don't be clever with me. I'll repeat the question. Do you know who I am?"

"No."

"Think hard. I know you can do better than that."

"You are the person who has committed the murders that Chief Sirsky is investigating."

"Congratulations. You can say Nico, don't you think? You have probably already slept with him."

There was silence. She wasn't going to get off so easily.

"So, did you sleep with him?"

"That is none of your business."

A wave of hatred rose inside him, drowning him like a tidal wave. It was no problem. He would take care of her later. He would take his time. He would play with her body. In the meantime, she needed to respect him. There was only one thing to do. He pulled the trigger, and the cop fell to the ground on his side, like deadweight. A red spot spread over his clothing. His eyes clouded over. He watched the hostages' reaction. Now the kid was frightened and was taking refuge against the woman. Fear had made its way into Caroline's eyes.

"What do you want?" she asked.

Now they were getting somewhere. He did not answer, ratcheting up the power he had over his prey. All he gave them was an icy smile.

"Don't do anything to him," she said.

"I'm not sure. It would feel like killing Nico Sirsky himself, and that could be a real rush."

"He's just a child."

"I admire your courage. I give in. There is rope and duct tape in my backpack. You are going to tie the boy to the table and make sure he can't scream. Do it right, or I'll have to kill him."

Caroline nodded and obeyed. The boy tried to resist, but she stopped him with a gesture. He looked at her anxiously. Tears were rolling down his cheeks. The man checked the knots and made sure the bonds would hold.

"Tell your father that I took his whore and am saving some of my very special treatment just for her. I'm sure he'll like that. Add that she is the seventh woman for the seventh day. Will you remember everything?"

The boy blinked in response. That was enough.

"Put your coat on. We're going," he ordered Caroline.

She did what he said without any fuss. She was afraid he would kill Dimitri. They left the house.

"Hold my arm, and look down."

They walked away without any trouble. He pushed her into his car.

"Perfect. Now don't move. I'll kill you at the first attempt to escape."

Now she was his.

SUNDAY

19

NIGHTMARES

He had never felt so weary before. He had never realized how his life was hanging by a thread. He was no longer in control. He was sitting on the edge of his bed, his face buried in Caroline's sweater, taking in her scent. He couldn't hold back the tears. He couldn't bear for her to suffer. He was so afraid of losing her. It was now impossible for him to imagine his future without this woman. He was tortured by the thought of her in that bastard's hands. He had to act. Time was of the essence. But what could he do? He felt a hand on his shoulder. He looked up. Magistrate Becker had come to join him.

"There was a time I didn't believe in anything anymore," Becker said. "But I clenched my fists, I moved forward, and I came out the other side. Each day that went by was a victory over fate. I loved my mother. She was everything to me. I was only seven years old. She was my universe. I watched her founder without being able to help her. Until she tried to kill me. My own mother. I had to rebuild everything, one brick at a time. I was able to rebuild my trust in other people, in my family. I have a wonderful wife who watches over our children like a jealous cat. The best can come from the worst, believe me. Nothing is set from the start. You know that better than anyone. The game is not over, Nico. You've got to keep playing to the end. Dr. Dalry is still alive, I'm sure of that. It's Sunday morning. The seventh woman for the seventh day, remember. He wouldn't have killed her yesterday. He's planning it this afternoon. This kind of person doesn't change his habits. Dominique Kreiss has confirmed that. We have a few hours in front of us. That's not a lot, but everything is still possible. Your team is waiting for your instructions. If you break, the whole system comes down with you. Nico? Let's fight this together. For her."

Nico looked deep in his eyes. So much had happened in so little time. The criminal had been leading them around all week. He had killed every day, and they hadn't managed to catch him. There weren't many psychopaths like this running around, but they were especially hard to apprehend. Now this one held Caroline, and she was the seventh pawn in his ghastly game. Everything had fallen into place quickly: the surgical gloves and the paper used in the medical examiner's offices, the discovery that the signature imprint on one of the messages belonged to Professor Vilars, the red campions crushed in the garden and the samples collected from the fifth victim, the shoe print on Captain Ader's skull, the contact lenses found in Fiori's office that were the same brand and correction as those found in Valérie Trajan's apartment, and the culprit's surgical knowledge. Finally, Marc Walberg compared the handwriting and confirmed that Eric Fiori wrote the messages.

A search of his home had provided irrefutable evidence. Deputy Chief Rost had gone there, as he had been ordered, and he had asked Nico to join him immediately. Fiori's wife was lying there, dead, the victim of the crime he had perfected. She was the sixth victim, a young brunette with a pleasant body, an accountant in a large Parisian firm. They had been married for four years and didn't have any children. He had written some words on the living room wall in red paint, "Let the lying lips be mute, for they speak arrogantly."

"Psalm 31, verse 18," Dominique Kreiss had said, Bible in hand, as they searched the premises.

The apartment was impeccable; everything was perfectly in order, revealing the occupant's obsessive nature. Eric Fiori had a den. Marine rope was coiled on the floor. A collection of knives was on display on one wall. On another wall was a collection of religious artifacts. A drawer was filled with bondage magazines. Bastien Gamby had joined them to examine the doctor's computer, where he found the victims' medical records that had come from their respective gynecologists. Then Gamby found traces of Nico's medical information, which the killer had gotten from the Saint Antoine Hospital network. It was enough to give them the chills.

Then the computer screen went fuzzy. Pulpy red lips appeared on it and broke into a sarcastic laugh. Nico understood immediately that the killer had planned everything. He wanted the investigators to end up in this apartment, so that they would hear the message he had for them. No, it was for him. Hadn't he been warned?

"Nico, I am shattering my enemies, and Sunday you will not rise. For her and the others, and for you, Nico, I'm preparing wickedness. I conceive mischief, and I bring forth falsehood. Can't you even protect your women, Nico? I am God. You are nothing."

From the second he saw those red lips on the computer, Nico knew he had lost, even before the metallic voice said a single word.

"I'm holding the seventh woman. I am going to undress her, torture her, and kill her. She is your woman, Nico."

And Caroline's picture took over the screen.

After that, he couldn't remember anything. What happened? How had he reacted? In the distance, he still heard Commander Kriven's voice trying to contact the police officers in charge of Dimitri and Caroline's safety. Less than a minute later, everyone was moving fast, taking him outside. They raced to his house. An officer lay soaked in his own blood inside the unmarked car, his carotid sliced open. Then they found his colleague, shot dead in Nico's apartment. His son was deathly pale. Nico cut him free, and Dimitri fell into his arms, not giving him the time to ask any questions.

"I couldn't do anything, Dad. I'm so sorry. I'm afraid for Caroline. She had to tie me up so that he wouldn't kill me."

A fleeting thought crossed his mind: He was grateful that it was she who had tied him up and not the killer.

"She's so strong, so calm," the teenager said. "I wasn't. She wanted him to leave me alone. She asked him to. She was brave. Dad, is he going to hurt her?"

He held Dimitri so tight, he almost smothered him.

"You're going to join Gran and Tanya," he said. "I'll take care of Caroline."

"She's, um, she's wonderful, Dad. Please find her. He wanted to know if she had slept with you."

"What?"

"That's what he said. And he said she was the seventh woman, that you'd know what that meant."

They took his son away. Nico was preoccupied with a single image: Caroline in the throes of death, nude and tied to the foot of a table, her skin whipped and lacerated. He swore he would kill Eric Fiori with his own hands.

The police forensics lab confirmed Alexandre Becker's innocence: His DNA had nothing in common with that of the presumed killer. Professor Charles Queneau had started comparing Dr. Fiori's DNA with the tissue samples on the contact lenses, the brown hair the criminal had left for them, and the mouth transfer Professor Vilars had found on the breasts grafted to Captain Ader. They would have the results in twenty-four hours, and that would be evidence against the criminal, along with the ear print found on Amélie Ader's door.

Some gray areas remained. Why was Eric Fiori killing these women? What was his story? Why thirty lashes for each victim? Nico had assigned some of his team members to the job of resolving that mystery. The others had been ordered to find out where Fiori could possibly go and where he could be hiding. In a few hours, Nico had the pathologist's full background. An only child, a middle-class family, divorced parents. Hard time in primary school and observations from a teacher who suspected abuse. An authoritarian mother who was prone to violence had died two years earlier under suspicious circumstances. Thieves had broken into her home and murdered her, according to the police report. Stabbed thirty times. Nico shivered. What if Eric Fiori had killed his mother? What had played out on that day? Fiori was the only one to have a key to that enigma. In a picture, his mother, around the age of thirty, looked surprisingly like the victims. So each time he committed the act, he was attacking his own mother. And he looked for prey that was like his mother. The pieces of the puzzle were coming together. Fiori had a studio apartment in Paris, rented to a student, and an apartment in Nice. Police sent to look there found nothing. There was nobody at Dr. Dalry's home, either. Where was he hiding? Where was Caroline? There were so many unanswered questions, despite all the detectives' efforts.

Feeling powerless, Nico wanted to go home. Becker and Kriven had gone with him. Night still enveloped the capital. Yellow flags flapped in the wind above the Samaritaine department store. Below, as on every other Sunday, the riverside roads were closed to cars and reserved for walking, roller skating, and biking. A joyful atmosphere reigned while he watched his entire existence collapse. Nico closed his eyes and let himself be driven home. He tried to quiet his anger and despair by reliving the feeling of Caroline's kisses and soft skin. He opened his eyes again and attempted to ignore the dull pain in his stomach. He had to save her, or else he would go mad.

Kriven finally parked the car. The three men went into the small house in the heart of the capital. He wanted to be alone, but he knew that his companions would not leave him. A few minutes later, he was sitting on his bed, burying his face in Caroline's sweater. Tears came to his eyes; he couldn't control it. That was when he felt Alexandre Becker's hand trying to reassure him. He admired this man, who had fought to survive and forget his past. Becker and Fiori had both experienced traumatic childhoods, but they had responded in completely opposite ways. Becker was right. He needed to fight.

"He's in Paris, that is for sure," Nico finally said. "We're watching all transportation out of the city. He couldn't risk fleeing the capital with Caroline. He'd be seen."

"I agree," Becker said. "And he'll follow the same modus operandi. These are symbolic acts for him."

"But we have no idea where he is!" Nico cried out.

"But there is a place."

"How can we find it? I'm taking the wrong approach."

"What do you mean?"

"He has become my enemy, and he knows what that means. To track a killer, you have to enter his world, perceive his urges, and follow him into the shadows."

"You mean empathize with him?"

"Exactly. Until you identify with him totally. There have to be clues that can lead us to him. I have to open my mind to find them."

Kriven had joined them in the room. "But we are talking about Caroline," he said. "That's what's upsetting you. You have to block your feelings and act as though she's someone you don't know, or you won't be able to do this."

There was a heavy silence.

"I thought that was bullshit," Becker said. "Barstool psychology."

"It depends on who does it," Kriven said. "Nico has a sixth sense for these things, even if he doesn't like to talk about it."

"He's been manipulating us from the beginning," Nico said.

"Except that he couldn't have planned that far ahead for Caroline," Kriven said.

"He wanted to attack my ex-wife, and then he discovered what was going on with Caroline and me. My sister, who knew him from the gym, let the cat out of the bag. Then he followed every step I made this week. Caroline came to headquarters. We walked together. She became his target. The truth is, everything was planned: a murder every day and the last one a culmination to take place today, Sunday. But it's his fantasies that feed his criminal ritual."

"Maybe his mother whipped him," Kriven said.

"Right. He is seeking revenge for that. For that matter, he most probably killed her. If his mother is the person he hates the most, and if he is trying to kill her through his crimes, then there is a close bond between her and the seventh and final victim," Nico said.

He has already stopped calling Caroline by name. He's back on track.

"He is holding his final prey," Nico continued. "What will he do with her? She has a special role in this game of his. He will probably inflict the same morbid ritual on her, but before, he used the victims' homes. This time, he has to change the way he does things. As meticulous and organized as he is, he has certainly prepared a place for his final exploit. It can't be just anywhere. Everything has to be perfect. Think about it. He has to escape from his mother. That's who the seventh woman is!"

"You mean that for him, the seventh woman is his mother?" Kriven asked.

"That's right. It wasn't enough to kill her once. He had to replay it. That's what he has been doing all week, but today, Sunday, it's the finale. A particular prey for a very special day. He wants to share his suffering with someone else, with someone he knows, and he has decided that I will be that person. He wants me to share the painful memory of his mother's death."

"He is totally crazy," Becker said.

"Where did his mother live?" Nico asked his commander. "Where did he grow up?"

"I don't know."

"Call Rost."

The deputy chief responded immediately. Everyone was on high alert. Kriven forwarded Nico's questions and waited a few minutes with the telephone glued to his ear.

"Three Place Jussieu, in the fifth arrondissement. Eric Fiori grew up there. His mother always lived in the same apartment, and she died there."

Kriven passed on this key piece of information to Nico.

"Tell Rost to meet us there, but to go quietly," Nico said. "I want to know the names of the present owners."

"Do you really think he could be there?" Kriven asked after hanging up.

"He's going back to his beginnings. That fits the killer's profile. He premeditated his mother's murder and went back to her place to follow his fantasy through to the end."

Nico left his home, with his two companions behind him. He was holding Caroline's sweater for reassurance. He climbed into the backseat of the car to give himself the space he needed to put himself in the killer's shoes. Kriven started the engine and headed toward Place Jussieu, where France's largest university stood. Pierre and Marie Curie University's modern buildings rose where there was once a wine market. The police commander took the Rue Jussieu and drove past the few buildings lining the square. It was crucial that they not be seen from the windows. Rost had taken the same route and was already there, his car double parked a little farther along. Théron and Vidal were there as well.

"It's on the third floor," Rost announced. "A retired couple bought the apartment from Fiori. There is only one door on each floor. There is a push-button system to enter the building."

"I've got the equipment we need in the trunk," Kriven said.

"Perfect," Nico said. "Let's go. I'll go first with Kriven. You follow along ten minutes afterward. Alexandre, you stay in the car."

The die was cast. Nico was sure Fiori and Caroline were there. He felt it deep inside. He couldn't be wrong; the woman's life depended on it. He advanced toward the building's entrance, with Kriven alongside him. The two men pinned themselves to the door, out of sight of the third-floor occupants. A large balcony shielded them. The commander opened his toolbox and took out the instruments he needed. He handled them skillfully, and they heard a click. Nico pushed the door open.

There was a tiled hallway, then a double glass door. They could take an elevator or a staircase covered with thick dark-green carpet. They chose the latter and began the climb. All was quiet. There was no sign of morning activity. Outside, dawn was having a hard time piercing the heavy clouds that were threatening rain. Second floor. The others were certainly entering the front door they had left open. Third floor. A reinforced door. Nico put his ear to the door, alert to the slightest echo of a voice, any unusual sound. There was nothing. And what if he were wrong? His throat was tight with anxiety. His heart was racing. In his mind, he saw Caroline's face. He surprised himself by praying that he would get her back, that he would finally be able to take her in his arms. What should he do? Shoot out the lock and run across the apartment? If it were the wrong apartment, and the killer and Caroline were not there, he could always apologize and get the owners' door fixed. If he were right, Fiori could kill Caroline in a fit of violence. Maybe it was a better idea to control the balcony and the windows, at the risk of being seen by the criminal. But time was short. The rest of the team was coming up to join them.

He stared at Kriven, a message in his look, and aimed his gun. He pulled the trigger. The silencer produced the muffled sound of a popped champagne cork. The lock gave. Kriven pushed the door open with his full weight. Nico felt as though he had left his body, as though he were watching a movie in slow motion. His intuition guided him, almost despite himself. He slipped in after the commander. The others followed. They had done this many times before and simply followed their reflexes. They needed to clear every room as quickly as possible.

Jean-Marie Rost found the couple's room. The stale smell struck him. A man and a women, both around seventy years old, lay on the bed, their eyes wide open, dead. Their bedclothes were covered in blood. The inspector recognized the knife wounds. The unfortunate couple had nothing to do with this story. Nico was right. Fiori had been here.

Pierre Vidal looked around the kitchen. He entered an adjoining pantry, used to store utensils and canned goods. He started when the coffee machine suddenly began dripping, and he nearly shot it out of reflex. He quickly realized that it had been programmed to go on. Nobody moved. The killer had reduced them all to an anxious silence. What about Dr. Dalry?

Once inside Joël Théron crossed the dining room, he went through the door farthest from the front entry. It led to a small room at the back of the apartment with a view of the interior courtyard. The room looked as though it got very little sunlight. An old sewing machine sat on a small, dusty worktable near a sofa. A mirror hung above an imposing fireplace. The shelves of a bookcase sagged under the weight of old books. All was silent. He noted nothing else. Maybe Nico had been wrong. Maybe Fiori never intended to come here, and the owners were away on a trip. The problem remained: where had he taken the seventh victim?

David Kriven was the one to enter the large, light-filled room directly in line with the dining room. An ornate early-twentieth-century desk stood near two French doors that looked over the Place Jussieu. There was a magnificent Napoleon II gaming table, framed by two mahogany English bookcases. But there was no sign of an evil presence and even less evidence of Caroline. He imagined the state Nico had to be in. What if they hadn't gotten there in time? What if he discovered her dead, like the others?

Nico had taken the double doors facing the entrance. He guessed that it led to the apartment's main room. He slowly turned the handle and saw the dark mass of a leather couch through the crack. This was the living room. He had been right. With a knot in his throat, he pushed open the doors with a steady movement. There was no light. The shutters were closed. Yet he saw a shape sitting in a chair and then the form of someone wedged into an armchair. Neither showed any sign of movement. It was as though time had stopped. He looked at the chair and took a step forward. Then he understood. Terror took hold of him. He lowered his weapon.

20

CAROLINE

"I could have chosen your ex-wife, but that wouldn't have had the same effect, would it?" Eric Fiori said in a merry voice. "Your sister. I thought about that very seriously. An attractive woman, but too blond for me. She did not fit, you understand? I had to make sure my victims fit the same profile, since that's what people expect of a serial killer, right? Tanya gave me the solution. She's the one who put me on the scent of the beautiful Caroline. It's your fault, in fact; if you hadn't fallen in love with her, she would be safe now. Did you fuck her? Was it good, Nico?"

Provoke him or play the game? Which was the better strategy? Nico heard his heart beating in his chest. Most important, he couldn't approach the criminal like an enemy, or he wouldn't be able to communicate with him. He had to convey empathy but not treat him like a friend. He had to get him to talk, listen to him, create a state of confusion in which the killer identified with him, the policeman, and vice versa. This would push the killer to pour out his feelings, but the cop was taking an enormous risk. Clearly, Fiori was extremely dangerous, and Nico realized that straight-forward understanding language would be the best weapon. This kind of criminal would be more destabilized by an attitude filled with tolerance rather than by angry words he had heard all too often.

"No, I haven't yet made love to this woman," he said calmly, hiding the worry that was eating away at him.

"Not yet? Poor Nico. So you'll never have the chance. You're crazy about her, aren't you?"

"I am."

"Bingo! You at least kissed her, didn't you?"

"Yes, several times."

"And what was it like?"

"I liked it."

"You wanted more, didn't you?"

"Yes."

"Good, good. I suggest that you set down your weapon now. You see, I'm pointing my gun at her, and I won't hesitate to pull the trigger, as you can imagine. I have nothing to lose."

Nico obeyed and set his gun down on the coffee table. His colleagues would be coming, drawn by the sound of voices.

"Here comes the cavalry," Fiori said. "Tell them not to try anything. They can turn the light on now."

"Do what he says," Nico ordered.

Kriven hit the switch, and light shot out of a superb Venetian glass chandelier. Fiori had risen from his chair and stood behind the young woman, his gun pressed against her temple. There was total silence. The police officers stared at the criminal without blinking.

"You've seen. Now clear out." Fiori sounded impatient. "Give your orders, Nico. I want them out of here. This is between me and you."

"Go on." Nico ordered his men out of the room.

"Are you sure?" Rost asked. "The owners were killed in their bed."

"He's sure," Fiori said. "Or it's his chick next. And leave your pieces here. You probably have other ones, but that means there won't be as many."

"Obey," Nico said in a firm voice.

His team members set their weapons down on the thick, cream-colored carpet and left the room. They closed the door behind them.

"I hope none of them are going to try to be smart," Fiori threatened.

"If anyone does, he'll have to deal with me," Nico interrupted.

They heard the men's footsteps trail off.

"So here we are, alone," the coroner said.

"Why?" Nico asked, having trouble looking away from Caroline.

"You can stare at her, Nico," Fiori said, watching him.

Caroline was sitting very straight, her hands tied behind the back of the chair, her skirt hiked up mid-thigh over skin-colored nylons, and her white silk blouse unbuttoned to offer a view of a lace bra. Duct tape across her mouth kept her from saying anything. Her face showed no emotion. She remained her own master, and a captivated Nico was impressed. Caroline's eyes expressed relief in knowing he was there, and he hoped he would be deserving of this trust.

"What did you do to her?" Nico asked, deciding to take a familiar tone.

"Not a thing, don't worry. I just touched her breasts. You know how much I love that part of a woman's body. But I put everything back in order, her bra and her shirt. Have you already played with her tits?"

"Yes," Nico said, his voice tight.

"You sound moved. They are soft, aren't they?"

Nico nodded. He wanted to throw himself at the sleazebag and bash him to death, but he had to be patient. He tried to relax and regain control of his breathing. He had to focus on the match. The end was near.

"Look. I brought my wife's breasts. They're in the jar. I thought I might have time to sew them onto the beautiful Caroline. But none of that is important anymore."

"Why?" Nico asked, feeling nauseous.

"Ah, why. Isn't that the big question. There always has to be a reason. Isn't that right? In any case, it's always easier to understand and more practical to forget. What if I just did it for the pleasure? The pleasure of dominating, humiliating, and butchering?"

"I don't believe that. There's something else."

"How disappointed you would be if I did it just for the enjoyment. You would think that all those women died for no reason, not even to fulfill a fantasy. You wouldn't have any explanation for the families. The unfairness of fate would pursue them to their last breath. But an explanation for my behavior would make their grieving easier. That's what you would like."

"The words on the wall mean something," Nico said, pointing to the message written quickly in still-fresh red paint.

"Read it."

"For my loins are filled with burning. And there is no soundness in my flesh."

"Psalm 38, verse 7."

"What is this burning, Eric?" Nico asked, managing to utter his name as if he were a friend.

"A dull, smoldering pain that the years have not erased."

"What did she do to you? What did your mother do?" Nico asked, alert for the tiniest movement, afraid he might trigger some anger.

"There we are, finally. The great motive that drives serial killers: hate for one parent or the other. Mostly for that dominating, castrating mother who traumatizes her child. Isn't that reassuring? It is so much easier to point to the mother or the father than to blame society and its ideologies. My mother—you *are* right, she was the first of all the bitches," Fiori said, his eyes closed to better see her ghost.

"Tell me. I want to understand. Why thirty lashes with the whip? Why always thirty?"

"An anniversary, of course. Of the day when, after hitting me, she raped me. But can a woman really force a man or, in my case, a male child? And did I enjoy the perverted game?"

"A child endures but does not decide. You had no responsibility in what happened."

"Perhaps. In any case, I took care of her."

"So it was you, then?"

"Stabbed her thirty times in her gut. It was sheer butchery, but what pleasure I felt. It's been exactly thirty years since she did that to me."

"And your father?"

"He didn't give a shit. He left the house and rebuilt his life without me. Another woman, other children. He chose to forget me and my crazy mother."

"A teacher raised suspicions."

"I see you studied my file. My mother shut her up quickly. Case dismissed."

"You never talked about this to anyone?"

"I was just a child. You're the one who said it."

"What do all these women have to do with it?"

"Nothing at all, Nico. Just fate. All they did was look like her. Same body, same presence. It must be that killing once was not enough for me."

"Don't you think that it's enough now? Can't you finally find peace with yourself?"

"I see where you are trying to go, Nico. You would like to save the beautiful Caroline. I haven't decided yet. In fact, I wanted to kill her like the others and then invite you to come see. I would have gotten off on that. I would have loved watching you discover her ravaged, lifeless body and seeing your pain. I would have wounded you forever. You would never have forgotten me, even if you put me away forever. I would have taken one more life:

yours. But I have to admit that you blew me away; you arrived earlier than I thought you would, and I had to change my plans. I'm angry, Nico. I wanted to kill her, and I did not have the time. So, we'll see. I'm still holding my gun, and I can pull the trigger whenever I want."

"I will kill you afterward."

"I don't give a damn, which is exactly why I am stronger than you. My life means nothing to me anymore."

"Caroline is innocent. She does not deserve to pay for what your mother did to you."

"Nico, do you know what a serial killer is? You don't need me to tell you. I relieve my suffering by taking innocent victims. I have a pattern. I'm sick. I do not feel the slightest remorse. And if you don't stop me, I'll start over again."

"I can't let you go. You know that."

"Even in exchange for Caroline's life, Nico? You would carry the burden of her death on your conscience."

The conversation was wearing Nico out, and his mouth was so dry, he was having trouble articulating.

"She is not like the others. She is not pregnant."

"That's true, but I decided not to care, as with Ader. Did you know that my mother got an abortion? I was six years old. There could have been two of us to fight her off."

"I love her, Eric. Don't kill her. I couldn't bear it."

"The mysteries of love, or is it sex? She is so attractive."

Nico once again tried to catch Caroline's eyes; he wanted to run up to her, untie her, take her into his arms, and get her to safety. Yes, he had loved this woman from the first minute he saw her, and he couldn't live without her.

"What's with the brown hair you left for us?"

"A little souvenir from my mother. Did you know that she did drugs too? Professor Queneau couldn't have missed that."

"Why did you use Dr. Perrin?"

"That scared you, didn't it? Tell the truth. The kind, inoffensive brother-in-law made up to look like a killer. You know, I went to his office several months ago, under a fake name, of course. He loves those fisherman's knots. All those picture boxes. I thought that would be fun, don't you agree? Okay, have I answered all your questions? Are you relieved? Now you can explain it to the families. 'He killed her, but he had been beaten and raped as a child. That is why.'"

"Becker's childhood was painful, as well, but he managed to overcome it. Your past does not excuse or justify your actions. All it does is explain them."

"Oh, oh! Now you are provoking me. Don't push me to the breaking point. It could cost you Caroline. That Becker thing is incredible, isn't it? I dug around in your professional circles to spice up the chase; there are always secrets to discover. I found a big one. Little Arnaud Briard stabbing his mother to death, and now he's Investigating Magistrate Alexandre Becker. What a career. In the end, he and I both took care of our mothers in the same way."

"For him, it was legitimate self-defense."

"You're playing with words, Nico. It was for me, too. Although I admit I was a few years late."

"He did not take out his revenge on the innocent."

"So maybe it's in the genes. You know the debate. Are you born a serial killer, or do you become one? It's difficult to say. The scientists are split. When I was a kid, I liked to cut off lizard tails. One night, I stuck a kitchen knife into my cat's belly, and then I got rid of the animal. I always had a thing for other people's suffering. When a child cried during recess, I watched and felt a kind of pleasure. Do you think I was born bad?"

"There is good inside every one of us."

"You're serving up religious bullshit. You can do better than that."

"I thought you were a Bible enthusiast."

"I haven't had any faith for a long time now. I used that to provoke."

"Whom?"

"You, the judge, Vilars, all of you."

"Professor Vilars?"

"The bitch. I would have gladly bedded her, but I wasn't good enough for her. And the way she looks at you. Are you even aware of it? She would eat you if she could."

"That's a little exaggerated."

"No, no. But it doesn't matter."

"Clearly you don't like women. What about your wife? You were married for several years."

"I had to look normal, didn't I? She was there, consenting, and I married her."

"You must have felt something for her, at least at the beginning, didn't you?"

"I'm going to disappoint you, Nico, but no, never. Killing her allowed me to get rid of her. I don't regret anything. Don't try to find the slightest remorse in me. That would be useless. I have chosen my fate."

"The future has not yet been written."

"All true. So, what would you be willing to do, to sacrifice even, to save Caroline's life? What is she worth to you?"

"Me. A trade."

"Sorry. I'm not interested in men. Not even your son. I could have taken him, though, you know? He looks so much like you. That would have been amusing. But you see, I barely even thought about it. I must admit that Caroline was convincing, pushing me to take her and leave him. Of course, I had come only for her."

"That is all I have to offer: me."

"What do you think she has to say about that? Let's ask."

Fiori slid his hand along the young woman's face and ripped off the duct tape, freeing her to talk. Caroline grimaced.

"So, Dr. Dalry," the killer said. "What do you think? Should I kill him in exchange for your life?"

"No."

He hadn't called her by her first name, and Nico realized how ill at ease he was with her, despite everything he was doing to hide it.

"Caroline, shut up!" Nico said.

"Ouch, a lover's quarrel," Fiori chuckled. "Already fighting, off to a bad start."

"If I'm the one you want, then force him to go away, and let's get this over with," Caroline said.

"Please, not that!" Nico threw her a chastening look.

"This is a real dilemma," Fiori said. "I'm going back and forth between the two of you."

His gun was still pointed at Caroline's temple. Nico had hoped he would lower his guard. If he tried anything rash, he risked losing everything. There was only one solution, to keep him talking, to play for time and find some weakness. But the minutes were passing, bringing them closer to an end he couldn't bear.

"Wait, I have a little idea that will help me think," the coroner said.

He thrust his hand down Caroline's shirt and fondled her breasts. Nico read disgust in the young woman's eyes and took a step forward, ready to swoop down on Fiori.

"Hey! Step back. I decide everything. You can't stop me. Be happy to watch. Imagine me cutting them off. How good that would be."

"She's not your mother, Eric. Leave her alone."

"My loins are filled with burning, and there is no soundness in my flesh," the criminal recited.

"Fight that burning!" Nico cried out in despair.

Fiori laughed and pulled his hand away from the woman's breasts. He looked truly demented and was losing control. Nico felt a quiver run down his spine. The killer straightened his arm, and Nico saw his finger tighten on the trigger.

"No," he threw himself forward with all his strength.

The shot burst like a bomb, ringing through the entire apartment and causing the walls to shake. Nico felt his muscles go weak, as though his legs were no longer holding him up. He was going to fall. Sweat dripped down his back. His thoughts went cloudy. The situation was out of his control. He was not that strong, after all. He was losing the round. Soon, he didn't have enough air, and he realized that he couldn't breathe. The room was spinning. The red letters danced in front of him, like a threat. But he was too late. He heard Caroline scream. He would never be able to prove to her how much he loved her.

THE 7ᵀᴴ WOMAN

The gunshot caused them all to jump. They had evacuated the building. Rost and Kriven were at the entrance to the apartment and were doing everything in their power to remain steady.

Caroline's scream made their blood run cold. Silence settled in. Outside, Théron and Vidal had climbed up to the balcony and were hiding behind the closed shutters. The old rusted panels would be easy to open. They were just waiting for orders from Rost. Thanks to his earpiece, Théron was in constant communication with his superior officer, and he could hear his breathing accelerate after the shot was fired. They had to try something. Fiori was crazy and wouldn't let Caroline and Nico out unharmed. Backup would be here any minute, but that might be too late. Who was the shot intended for?

"Can you get into the room?" Rost whispered into Théron's ear.

"Yes."

"Good, go ahead. Quietly. Kriven and I will go in the door."

Théron signaled to Vidal, who nodded, clearly relieved. Théron broke the hooks that held the shutters closed and opened them quietly. The two then went in, passing the elderly couple lying stiff on the bed. They advanced, the carpet muffling their footsteps.

At the front, Rost gently pushed the door open. He looked through the crack, making sure that Fiori hadn't spotted him. Behind him, Kriven waited impatiently. Gripping their weapons, they stole into the apartment. They had agreed on the best way to corner the killer. The most worrisome part was the heavy silence. What was happening? Were Nico and Caroline still alive?

§ § §

Becker couldn't stand it anymore. It was unbearable to be there, pacing around the police car. Even if he couldn't intervene, he felt involved. Hadn't the killer provoked him by revealing his secret and making him the ideal suspect? But most of all, he was thinking about Chief Sirsky. That man, who had seemed so cold and sure of himself, had become likable. This case had brought them closer, and the nascent friendship he felt for him was shared. He couldn't stand the thought that a killer could challenge a policeman and threaten the woman he loved. But his worry was mixed with hope. These policemen were the best France had. They would come through this. Or else there was no justice.

§ § §

Caroline's eyes were filled with tears. Her lips were trembling. Her face was pale. The bonds were hurting her. Yet she was sitting straight, as if to confront the situation better. She was magnificent, and right to the end, he would fight for her. He clenched his teeth, staying on his feet and challenging the pain that was asphyxiating him. Blood was streaming down the leg the bullet had penetrated. This was not the first time he had been a target, but it was the first time he had been hit, and it was at close range.

"Congratulations!" Fiori mocked. "Chief Sirsky in the role of the strapping, courageous hero. So, doctor, were you afraid? He wanted me to shoot him over you so much, I couldn't let him down."

"You bastard," Nico muttered. "You'll pay for this."

"But I don't give a damn! Give me a single good reason to continue living."

"Let her go."

"No way. Did I tell you about Captain Ader? No? You should have seen the look on her face when she realized. She defended herself well, better than the others. She made things a little difficult for me. She suffered terribly, as you can well imagine. She kept her head on longer than the other girls. A real pleasure."

"You make me sick!"

"Now, now, control yourself."

"You son of a bitch."

"Stop."

"You only attack the weak. You've got no balls."

"Stop it right now, or I'll hit your other leg."

"I'm sure you never gave a woman any pleasure. A premature ejaculator, right? What did your wife think about that? She didn't get enough, did she? Maybe she looked somewhere else."

"You're stupid. I'm going to kill you."

"Is that so? You think you're God, but you're just a shit. A dirty fucking bastard."

Caroline's opened her eyes wide with incomprehension. Nico was wounded. He was losing blood, and that upped the pressure. She was afraid he was putting himself in too much danger. She didn't want the killer to shoot him again. If she could just get his attention.

Create a diversion to protect Nico. Tip the chair over and fall to the floor. The killer would be furious, and that was exactly what she wanted. He would target her, which would give Nico the small opportunity to react. The tension was so high, a single movement could cause a tragedy.

They all heard what was being said. They understood immediately that Nico had changed his strategy. Because empathy hadn't worked, and time was of the essence, he had decided to attack the killer head-on. It was dangerous, but he didn't have a choice. They needed to be ready to intervene. Maybe Nico would give them a signal. He knew that his team was still there and ready to jump in, weapons in hand. There was no going back.

"And you know what?" Nico shouted. "I lied to you earlier. I fucked Caroline. She was great. But she's not for you. You couldn't play with her the way you played with the other women. You're pathetic. In the end, I'm the one who fooled you."

The blood drained from Fiori's face. He grimaced in disgust. Nico had stung him.

"Armelle Vilars never wanted to sleep with you. She told me," Nico said. "It made her laugh that you wanted her. She was sure you were a bad lay. You are a bad lay, Fiori! A sexual neurotic! A loser who doesn't know how to make a woman come. An incompetent. You prefer to tie them up and stare at them."

"Shut up! Shut up, or I'll kill her."

"Is that so? And what if you started with me?"

"You're pissing me off, Sirsky."

"You're not calling me by my first name anymore, Fiori? Are we no longer friends? You're right. I've got nothing in common with a dirty slimeball like you."

Nico felt he strength draining from him. His only goal was to try everything he could before it was too late. His men were there; he knew it. He just had to say the word, and they would spring into the room. The moment was nearing. It was a gamble. But he trusted his team. They would respond, or he would die with Caroline. Thoughts of Dimitri filled his mind. Did he have the right to abandon his son? What would he become? Had he told him that he loved him enough times? Had he told him how proud he was of the man he was becoming?

There was doubt on the killer's face. He needed to gather his thoughts. Nico knew that he had to keep up the pressure

"I've figured it out! Your fucking mother made you impotent! That's it. Go ahead. Say it."

The weapon was pointing at him. Fiori was about to shoot when the chair started tipping and fell on its side. Nico desperately tried to catch Caroline's eyes. She had distracted the killer.

"Go!" Nico yelled when a second shot rang out.

That was the signal.

Kriven shouldered the door violently and threw his body forward. He spotted Fiori and shot without hesitation. At the same time, Rost burst into the living room with Théron and Vidal behind him. Dr. Dalry was lying on the ground; it was impossible to tell if she was dead. He saw that Nico was still standing. Fiori had the chief in his sights. Rost pulled the trigger.

Nico kept his balance for a moment. The truth was that he could no longer feel his leg. But he couldn't say where the second bullet had hit. He felt pulled. He wanted to apologize to his entire family, to his son, and to Caroline, too. If he hadn't crossed paths with her, she would never have been part of this tragedy. Would she ever manage to forget? He hoped so.

Two more shots shook him, stirring the air around him. His leg gave out. He collapsed. He stared at Fiori as he was falling. The killer swayed, his eyes wide with surprise. Two blood stains spread across his sweater. Two wounds. He toppled backward, as if in slow motion, and hit the floor, smashing a group of crystal vases that had been set there by the elderly tenants.

He tried to keep a grasp on reality. He saw Caroline wriggle to undo the ropes. She crawled over to him on her knees. She examined him and shouted out incomprehensible orders. She was calling him back to life.

His men were moving around him. They slapped him on the face, not holding back. He preferred the young woman's touch. She was alive.

The son of a bitch would not have his seventh woman. He felt happy. The outline of the bodies leaning over him blurred. The voices became more distant. As in a dream, he imagined his son, that baby he had held tenderly in his arms. Everything started accelerating. There he was running at his side, telling him how to steer his bike. Multicolored balloons were flying overhead. He heard Dimitri's laughter ring out. His son encouraged him to grab the yellow one, the blue one, the red one, the green one. He was calling him back to life.

Was he going to die?

No, not now that he had Caroline.

He would fight.

Thank you for reading The 7ᵗʰ Woman.

We invite you to share your thoughts and reactions on Goodreads and your favorite social media and retail platforms.

We appreciate your support.

About the Author

Writing has always been a passion for Frédérique Molay. She graduated from France's prestigious Science Po and began her career in politics and the French administration. She worked as chief of staff for the deputy mayor of Saint-Germain-en-Laye and then was elected to the local government in Saône-et-Loire. Meanwhile, she spent her nights pursuing the passion she had nourished since penning her first novel at the age of eleven. After *The 7th Woman* took France by storm, Frédérique Molay dedicated her life to writing and raising her three children. She has five books to her name, with three in the Paris Homicide series.

About the Translator

Anne Trager has lived in France for more than twenty-six years, working in translation, publishing, and communications. In 2011, she woke up one morning and said, "I just can't stand it anymore. There are way too many good books being written in France not reaching a broader audience." That's when she founded Le French Book to translate some of those books into English. The company's motto is, "If we love it, we translate it," and Anne loves a good police procedural.

About Le French Book

Le French Book is a New York-based publisher specializing in great reads from France. As founder Anne Trager says, "There is a very vibrant, creative culture in France. Our vocation is to bring France's best mysteries, thrillers, novels, and short stories to new readers across the English-speaking world."

www.lefrenchbook.com

DISCOVER MORE BOOKS FROM

LE FRENCH BOOK

The Paris Lawyer by Sylvie Granotier
A psychological thriller set between the sophisticated corridors of the Paris courts and a small backwater in central France, where rolling hills and quiet country life hide dark secrets.
www.theparislawyer.com

The Winemaker Detective Series
by Jean-Pierre Alaux and Noël Balen
A total Epicurean immersion in French countryside and gourmet attitude with two expert winemakers turned amateur sleuths gumshoeing around wine country. Already translated: *Treachery in Bordeaux, Grand Cru Heist* and *Nightmare in Burgundy.*
www.thewinemakerdetective.com

The Greenland Breach by Bernard Besson
The Arctic ice caps are breaking up. Europe and the East Coast of the United States brace for a tidal wave. A team of freelance spies face a merciless war for control of discoveries that will change the future of humanity.
www.thegreenlandbreach.com

The Bleiberg Project by David Khara
Are Hitler's atrocities really over? Find out in this adrenaline-pumping ride to save the world from a conspiracy straight out of the darkest hours of history.
www.thebleibergproject.com

NOV 22 2014

POP

CPSIA information can be obtained at www.ICGtesting.com
Printed in the USA
BVOW03s1555030614

355225BV00003B/4/P

once you've started it, and we are hoping that Frédérique Molay writes many more like it."

—*RTL*

"A slick, highly realistic, and impeccably crafted thriller. Likeable characters, outstanding pacing, and unexpected plot twists that keep readers guessing throughout...an extraordinary, hard-hitting novel."

—*ForeWord Reviews*

"Author Frédérique Molay does a superb job of building the suspense in overt and subtle ways...Don't pick this book up unless you're planning to read for a while because, I assure you, you won't be able to put it down."

—*Criminal Element*

"The plot has plenty of twists and dead ends to keep you guessing and entertained: it certainly had me reading until late at night. But what I really liked about the books are the realistic and workman-like descriptions of the police investigation...All in all, an enjoyable, solid police procedural, which proves you can sustain suspense without going overboard on thrillerish elements."

—*Finding Time to Write*

"It is a handsomely written and wonderfully translated Parisian police procedural that also will prowl your mind...The ugly parts are appalling, but Molay has the prowess to touch lightly upon them before exploring the horror seeping into the hardened police ranks."

—*Durango Herald*